The Publication
of Poetry and Fiction
A Conference

Held at the Library of Congress,
October 20 and 21, 1975

Library of Congress   Washington   1977

Library of Congress Cataloging in Publication Data

The Publication of poetry and fiction.

  Sponsored by the Gertrude Clarke Whittall Poetry and Literature Fund.
  Bibliography: p.
  1. Publishers and publishing—United States—Congresses. 2. Authors and
publishers—United States—Congresses. I. United States. Library of Congress.
II. United States. Library of Congress. Gertrude Clarke Whittall Poetry and Liter-
ature Fund.
Z479.P83   070.5'0973   77-608008
ISBN 0-8444-0233-8

This conference was presented by the Gertrude Clarke Whittall Poetry and Literature Fund with the additional support of a grant from the National Endowment for the Arts.

The Gertrude Clarke Whittall Poetry and Literature Fund was established in the Library of Congress in December 1950 through the generosity of Mrs. Gertrude Clarke Whittall (1867-1965) to create a center in this country for the development and encouragement of poetry, drama, and literature. Mrs. Whittall's earlier benefactions include the presentation to the Library of a number of important literary manuscripts, a gift of five magnificent Stradivari instruments, the endowment of an annual series of concerts of chamber music, and the formation of a collection of music manuscripts that has no parallel in the Western Hemisphere.

These proceedings are published by the Library to reflect the state of the art of literary publishing as seen by some of its prominent practitioners and advocates.

Contents

Welcoming Remarks

The Acting Librarian of Congress

Good morning, ladies and gentlemen, and welcome to the Library of Congress. I am John Lorenz, the acting Librarian, and I'm very pleased to welcome you here on this cool, crisp day in Washington where you can see forever. There aren't too many days like this anymore, and we hope that the ideas and deliberations that come forth from this conference will be cool and clear and farseeing, also. The central concern of this conference, as you know, is the publication problem facing authors and publishers of poetry and serious fiction in the United States. The Library of Congress is deeply concerned about this problem, and we are pleased to provide a forum for its investigation and ideas for its solution. I also want to take this opportunity to express the Library's appreciation to the National Endowment for the Arts, whose support has helped make this conference possible. Over the next two days I expect you will find areas of agreement and disagreement. We hope that your deliberations and ideas will be influential—first upon the group gathered for the conference, and second, through publication of the proceedings, upon a wider audience throughout the United States.

Authors, publishers, and librarians, I believe, coexist in a symbiotic relationship. The author's work has no effective existence until it secures publication. Publication implies distribution and dissemination to a reading public, large or small. And libraries, in fulfilling responsibility to select, acquire, preserve, and make available, are among the chief purchasers of some titles issued in small editions. Poetry and serious fiction are often in that number, but it cannot be conducive to a healthy cultural life when a publication's success is almost completely dependent upon institutional rather than individual purchase. And in an era when the resources available to libraries may continue to decline in purchasing power, such a dependence is misplaced. So it is in the interest of this Library, therefore, and of all libraries, that there be an increase in the reading public for contemporary creative literature—an increase evidenced by the willingness of individuals to buy and

1

read serious fiction—and I trust that this conference will contribute substantially to that result. And now, to lead us on the way,
I'm very pleased to turn the program over to the general chairman for the conference, the Library's consultant in poetry and
our good friend, Stanley Kunitz.

Trade Publication

Peter Davison, chairman; Jonathan Baumbach; James Laughlin; Frances McCullough; Diane Matthews; Betty Prashker; Richard Seaver

Stanley Kunitz:

On behalf of the Poetry Office, welcome. That includes the panelists, too.

I'd like to say a few words about the reason for planning this conference and the motives behind it. Last spring I sent a memorandum to John Broderick, chief of the Manuscript Division, under whose aegis the Poetry Office operates, and in that memo I discussed the plan for a conference of this nature. The object, as I put it then—I have the memo in front of me—was to discuss current conditions in the book world relative to acceptance in publishing of poetry manuscripts and to suggest ways and means of stimulating publishers' interest in poetry and in reaching a larger audience. And in the note that followed, the following paragraph appears:

> The publishing industry considers itself to be in a "state of crisis." At a recent meeting of the American Association of Book Publishers' General Book Division, discussion focused on the need to eliminate marginal books, and those that sell less than 5,000 copies. Several publishers have already cut back on their poetry lists, among them Harper & Row and Doubleday. Atheneum, which has been in the forefront of poetry publishing, is no longer reading unsolicited poetry manuscripts. Six university presses have abandoned poetry: Columbia, Cornell, Indiana, Chicago, Hawaii, and Nebraska. Even established poets are experiencing difficulty finding publishers.

As you can see from this note, the original intention was to confine discussion to the state of poetry publishing, but at the valuable suggestion of the National Endowment for the Arts, which generously supplied a grant to help fund the conference, the program has been expanded to include consideration of the almost equally sad state of affairs with respect to the publishing of fiction.

Back in 1932, W. H. Auden asked a question that has reverber-

3

ated through the following decades: "What do you think about England, this country of ours where nobody is well?" Most publishers, I think, who care about literature—and there are some who do—and nearly all serious writers, if asked the same question about the condition of the American publishing industry, would have to reply in much the same way: "Indeed, it is not very well."

I'd like to summarize briefly a few recent developments that are relevant to our discussion. The 1976 summer issue of *Coda*—the newsletter of Poets & Writers, Inc.—reported that for 1975 and 1976, several major publishing houses are planning severe cutbacks in the total number of books they plan to publish. Items: Macmillan is cutting its total list by over 30 percent; Scribner's is cutting its list by about 30 percent; Viking's planned offerings are down about 20 percent; Random House plans a cutback of about 10 percent, and so on. One publisher is quoted as saying that the current publication list of major publishers will be cut back about 30 percent by the end of the year, in general throughout the trade. You might ask what's so serious about that, especially in a year that's seen the publication of four definitive biographies of Judy Garland. Maybe it might be a good idea to cut back on the publication of some of those books, but, unfortunately, what that involves is the elimination of serious writing. It really means the elimination, to a degree at least, of the publishing of poetry and fiction—particularly first novels and certainly short stories. There's a paragraph in *Coda* that explains that. It says:

> Fiction and poetry are expected to be hurt the most despite the fact that they make up only a small fraction of the country's total book output. Fiction accounts for less than 10 percent, and poetry's share is so small that it is not even listed separately in Bowker's annual book survey. It appears there in combination with drama. At the most recent booksellers' convention, the following dialogue was reported:
>
> Bookseller: Too many books are published; why not cut back on the total?
> Publisher: If you eliminated one thousand books, you would exclude all the good ones, and be left with the schlock.

That's one publisher's answer.

Here's another item about novels that I think is of interest and will be of particular interest to this panel. In the last year, the number of first novels published has been reduced by half. In 1974, only about 120 first novels were published as compared to over 200 in 1973. And then there is an analysis of all the difficulties of distributing fiction and the serious problem of the returns that seem to bring back to the publisher most of the fiction that has been printed.

The conclusion, and it's a grim one, is this: authors of poetry and first fiction, none of whom are able to make a living from their books, will have minimal outlets for their work. This is a prophecy, and, as I said, it's a sour one. Some may be able to turn to the small presses and publishing co-ops, but these are run at low cost by the authors themselves and represent a precarious labor of love. Perhaps much of contemporary literature will go underground and be published in mimeograph for a handful of friends; or maybe, out of sheer concern, federal and state arts council money will buoy publishers in publishing low-interest books, set up purchase plans, and create distribution channels to reach the natural audience for contemporary writers at last.

I think that we are assembled here today and tomorrow to do more than discuss merely the economics or logistics of book publishing. What we are really discussing is the survival of the life of the imagination. And now I'd like to introduce the chairman of the first panel, the panel of trade publishers, largely. The chairman is someone I consider to be a dear friend—and he'd better be, because he's also my publisher—and I know that he is a man of varied talents, aside from being director of the Atlantic Monthly Press. He is himself a poet, has published several books of poetry, was a winner of the Yale Series of Younger Poets Award, and has published a memoir. He's one of those publishers who do care about literature. And now I give you Peter Davison.

Peter Davison:

Standing here to begin this conference is a little bit like being present at some extraordinary ritual at which people gather around for the opening of the largest can of worms in the world. My title in talking about trade publishing of poetry and serious fiction is "An Imaginary Business." Publishing is indeed a business, but, insofar as it deals with the publishing of poetry and serious fiction, it is imaginary. Perhaps it should be. My epigraph is from one of my favorite contemporary laws—my two favorite contemporary laws: the first is Murphy's Law, which is, "If anything can go wrong, it will"; and the second is Price's Law, which is a little more applicable to publishing and the world: "If everybody doesn't want it, nobody gets it."

One of my firm's most highly prized authors, Francis Steegmuller, wrote me lately to say: "I join you in wishing for a world in which novels will outsell cookbooks." As a *parti pris* I would have liked to have added "and where poetry will outsell novels." Whether we are poets and novelists or publishers—those natural enemies, vital like predator and herbivore to one another's survival—we would, I am sure, be happier to live in a world where poetry outsold novels and novels outsold cookbooks. But there is this little matter of natural enmity. The author as artist is the most individual of individuals, who can "see a world in a grain of sand." The publisher, however, represents the world of collectivity. William Blake was unusual among great writers in acting as his own publisher. In *The Marriage of Heaven and Hell* he wrote, "Opposition is true friendship." But, since he was his own publisher, it is interesting to note that this observation is obliterated in some copies of the original.

It may seem simplistic to state at the outset that trade publishing is part of American business, the private sector. Though I do have my reservations, I am happy enough to declare myself content with that situation, to feel that money is not out of place in the discussion, and that it is fair for author and publisher to divide the profits from publishing—when there are profits. The principal trouble with the publishing of poetry and new fiction is that there are few or no profits. If there were, we would not be here. I am afraid, then, that one has to look at the publishing of poetry and new fiction as an imaginary business; there is nothing businesslike about it. It remains to be seen, however, whether there is anything very businesslike about publishing itself.

Since at least 1945 American business has been obsessed with the perpetual achievement of "growth." The results are unmistakable: we have won the capacity to produce increasing quantities and varieties of goods and to find buyers for most of them. Publishing has not been immune. In the year I took my first publishing job—1950—13,000 books were published in the United States. In 1974, according to the annual count in *Publishers Weekly*, 40,846 titles were published. Of the 30,745 "new" books, 2,382 were fiction titles and 1,155 were new works of poetry or drama, and, as Stanley has pointed out, the two are indistinguishable. So we are concerned about 3,537 titles of fiction, poetry, and drama—less than 10 percent of all the books published in the United States last year. Perhaps that statistic by itself proves how deeply publishers are committed to what is generally known as the cultural life. But I'd like to suggest further that the vast increase of the last twenty-five years has visibly coarsened the fiber as well as swollen the output.

Nobody seems to consider sufficiently where the parabolic curve of growth might take us—the ghastly side effects on people used up and thrown aside, resources laid waste for the sake of quantitative expansion, talents lacerated by being wrested to unnatural tasks, economic and political strategies dumped overnight. There are those who will remember how the verb *to waste* was used by American soldiers in Vietnam.

When man first gathered into urban society ten thousand years ago, the work of the artisan developed into craftsmanship. Later merchants arose to engage in the acquisition, storage, and distribution of goods and the transformation of commodities and artifacts into wealth by barter or sale. Others—priests, servants, healers, barbers, midwives, prostitutes, and poets—began to perform services in behalf of the health of an identifiable constituency. Finally, very recently, some workers found themselves further specialized into managers, coordinating production and services for the sake of power and wealth. The modern manager is not concerned with craftsmanship, acquisition, distribution, or service—not primarily. He likes to say things like "My business is people."

For the modern manager the artifact turns into an abstraction and earnings become the reality. Most large corporations, as John Kenneth Galbraith has noted, cannot any longer be thought of as *making* anything at all, no identifiable product. And a favorite pose of management today is that publishers are no longer engaged in anything so primitive as printing and selling books. They think of themselves as "in the communications business"—a phrase which communicates very little.

Now the writer of fiction and poetry is nothing if he is not a craftsman; his official relationship to society comes through his constituency of readers or listeners. To reach them he puts himself into the hands of the publisher. The modern publisher, impressed—as the writer is not—by the advances in technology of recent decades, tries to emulate the efficiencies of the great industrial world. But for the dissemination of lyric poetry or the Bildungsroman, such techniques are absolutely useless. The economy of scale does not apply.

In the last two decades management has taken publishing away from the people we think of as publishers. The first step came with the huge expansion of textbook publishing to accommodate the postwar baby boom. Next came the transition to computer billing, shipping plants programmed by punch cards, and so on. Management soon realized that such warehouses were best suited to dealing rapidly and efficiently with huge quantities of a single item, like textbooks and bestsellers. Accountants, warehousemen, and salesmen who realized this prospered. Those who did not sought different lines of work. Publishing had involved another constituency to go with the reading public: those insentient computers at the warehouse.

Such techniques could not be adopted without radically changing management's way of making decisions. Still further touch was lost with the identity of the product, the book itself, and managers began living more than ever like the prisoners in Plato's cave, bewildered by the numbered shadows of indistinguishable items. One famous publisher greeted authors he met on the stairs with a nationally recognized grin and said to one and all, "We're very high on your book," and descended the staircase smiling.

In the last few years publishing costs have skyrocketed because of the increased costs of our vanishing raw materials. Worldwide inflation has pushed prices farther. But we often overlook the unaccountable costs of rationalization: management has set aside the craftsmanship of editors, designers, papermakers, printers, binders, and publishers. They have been forced to pay their workers the cost of indignity, to reward them in money for the lost satisfactions of serving a constituency, and, in addition, to pay the price of our inflated expectations as consumers of cars and refrigerators. What's more—and many of you may not believe this—the profits of general publishers have been decreasing. Why does management do it? Because the pressure towards growth is stronger than the pressure towards health or survival. Growth everywhere forces management towards incorporation, capitalization, and conglomeration. When computers come into style, managers must have computers or hang for it. When the style swings to bartering independence for tax advantages, the founders of publishing firms like Knopf; Random House; Harcourt, Brace; Little, Brown; Houghton Mifflin; Putnam; Dutton; Simon & Schuster; William Morrow, and others find it easier to give up their independence than their estates. Managers flock as irrationally as lemmings to hurl themselves into conglomerates which sell computers, TV sets, photocomposition, photocopying, and other electronic marvels. Firms like Xerox, RCA, IBM, CBS, Time, Inc.—all of whom now own publishing houses—may be miracles of modern corporate enterprise, but we have little reason to call them publishers.

New technological capacities offer endless opportunities for managerial flimflam. Governmental tax policies support the managerial revolution by encouraging owners of small companies to convert their holdings into shares of stock in large ones. An expanding population places a burden heavier than ever on the capacity for wide and rapid distribution. The mandate that falls on advertising to encourage undiscriminating consumption raises the economic expectations of the entire population and entices us all with the rewards of mass production, the denominators of mass taste, and the susceptibility to "media events." If a book doesn't blossom early as a media event, the chances are that management will shortly allow it to wither into a non-happening: "If everybody doesn't want it, nobody gets it."

Marshall McLuhan has written:

It is important to notice that none of the effects of technology are ever foreseen or desired. . . . Whenever a new form creates an environment that encompasses an old service, the older service becomes an art form. Gutenberg hushed the schoolmen but retrieved pagan antiquity on a scale unknown in the ancient world. . . . Electric circuitry may have phased out the assembly line, but it has retrieved the inner life and the occult.

Perhaps he is right. Perhaps that is why we are here, with our concern for the inner life, to discuss and dispute the conflicts between publishers and writers. Perhaps the very publication of writing that issues from the inner life, since it is an imaginary business, has nothing left but to flower into an art form. Maybe that's what's happening. If this is true, publishing will need finer artists, fewer managers or none, dedicated craftsmen, a heightened sense of responsibility to its constituency, and a healthy distaste for overrationalized production, electronic processing, mass distribution, and media events. (I hope it will also eschew such *truly* imaginary business as the spectacle of McGraw-Hill tooling up to publish a nonexistent title by Clifford Irving, an imaginary biographer, about Howard Hughes, a chimerical subject.) Publishing has a long way to go to recover its sense of reality, to act responsibly in bringing new imaginative writing to the public, and to dignify the arts both of literature and of publishing.

These are by way of opening remarks, with which I am sure some of the panelists here disagree violently. I'd like to introduce, from left to right, Richard Seaver of the Viking Press, Diane Matthews of Doubleday, Frances McCullough of Harper & Row, Betty Prashker of Doubleday, Jonathan Baumbach of the Fiction Collective, and James Laughlin of New Directions Publishers. I'm going to ask these ladies and gentlemen to respond in any way they wish to my remarks, and then, after they're through, we'll be open to questions from the floor. I'll begin with Mrs. Prashker.

Betty Prashker:

Good morning. I don't know why you all are lucky enough to have two representatives from the firm of Doubleday at the Library of Congress, but you have. I work for Doubleday. On the letterhead it says "Doubleday & Company, A Communications Corporation." I am, I hope, not a harbinger of gloom. I am not a prophet of gloom. I really don't agree with many of the things that my colleague Peter Davison has told you.

Publishing serious fiction and poetry may be a crazy business, but I don't think it's an imaginary business. If it is an imaginary business in the case of fiction, there are an awful lot of people who want to get into it, and I'm speaking of writers. We are deluged by manuscripts of novels that come in day after day after day, solicited and unsolicited. We try to give them as much attention as we possibly can, and I would say, without hesitation, that every manuscript that has some value to it is cheerfully considered. And I would go further than that, and this is where I may get quite a lot of disagreement. I don't think that any fiction manuscript that is good doesn't get published. I think a lot of junk gets published, but I also think that a lot of good things get published. It may take a long time for something to get published. It might take years, but eventually a piece of fiction that is serious, exciting, and good by any ordinary standard of values gets published. That's observation number one.

Observation number two, on the question of Judy Garland and four definitive biographies. Maybe two of them were definitive biographies, but I won't argue with that. Anyway, how definitive can you get about Judy Garland? There's always going to be something more to say about her. But I would say that at least two of those books, because of their potential for mass sales and for profits, have paid for some of the serious fiction that does get published by a large publishing house. This happens to be a fact.

Now Mr. Kunitz talked about a natural audience for contemporary fiction. This is a very interesting phrase. What is the natural audience for contemporary fiction? Are there ten thousand people out there somewhere who want to read what we're talking about, serious fiction, whatever that is? Because we must have ten thousand people buy the books in order to make that book, *qua* book, a viable publishing procedure for us. When we've sold ten thousand copies, we've made a profit. If we don't sell those ten thousand copies, we have not made a profit. Now, many times we have published books that we have considered to be serious fiction. We have promoted and advertised those books, and we've not found that natural audience. On the other hand, we have published a number of books of serious fiction, and we have found that audience, and we have gone beyond that audience. One example that I can think of is a marvelous book we published by Hannah Green which perhaps some of you read. It was called *The Dead of the House*; it was a first novel. Some of it had been published in the *New Yorker*. It received extremely good reviews, and it sold twenty thousand copies. It was sold into paperback as well and was picked up by a book club. This is serious fiction, it's also profitable fiction, it's also good fiction.

I think Mr. Davison is unnecessarily gloomy about the kinds of fiction being published. I think a publishing industry that can publish books, such as *Dog Soldiers* by Robert Stone, *Ragtime* by Ed Doctorow, *Gravity's Rainbow* by Thomas Pynchon, the Leonard Michaels book of short stories, Saul Bellow's novel, a new novel by Larry Woiwode, Joyce Carol Oates, John Gardner—you know I could go on indefinitely—publishes serious fiction, some of them achieving bestsellerdom, because they reach out somehow into an audience that is willing to buy the book and to recommend the book.

Now, I would say one other thing about serious fiction. A lot of times, when people talk about that, they seem to be talking about experimental fiction, and just because something is experimental, to me, doesn't mean it's good. There's just as much schlock experimental fiction as there is schlock narrative fiction, just to use a phrase, and I am not impressed by the argument that recites that experimental fiction doesn't have an audience. It doesn't have an audience because people don't want to read it if it isn't good. It's just as boring as anything else.

Finally, I have not mentioned anything about poetry because my colleague Diane Matthews, who's in charge of our poetry program, will speak to you about that. But I would like to end up by saying it's not as bad as they're telling you it is. If you write something good, it's going to get published, and chances are it's going to be noticed.

Davison:

Thank you. Next, Jonathan Baumbach of the Fiction Collective, himself a novelist, will speak.

Jonathan Baumbach:

I'm here, I think in a way, as a token writer. I was, by and large, ready to say something else until Mrs. Prashker spoke, so I'm going to change what I had to say, which I think is nice. At least there'll be some controversy.

I had an opportunity, a little bit ago, to look through *Publishers Weekly*'s fall offerings, and I was astonished. Beyond some of the titles, say, that Mrs. Prashker mentioned—which are, I think, prated to us as a form of tokenism, the serious fiction writer as celebrity—these books are selling because of the cachet, by and large, of a number of the writers. Tom Pynchon's *V.*, I think, is a very good example. I think there's a club of about twenty-seven people who've read it through—though I think it's a very good book, and I'm glad it's published. There's hardly a book coming out in the fall, that I can see, that an intelligent person would want to read. I think that the schlock drives out serious fiction very much the way Gresham's law ostensibly operates, and the serious fiction that comes through gets published for other reasons, and not to say, I think by and large that publishers are behaving with good intentions. I think they were probably positively philanthropic to us in the old days, when it was a business with considerably more pride and generosity—I should say very much concerned with the quality of books. And I think that's inevitably changed.

It bothers me, though, the myth that all good fiction is getting published, because I know it's not true. I think the corollary of that is that good fiction has a reasonable-sized audience, and I think there's a kind of obvious contradiction going on. There's no reason why good fiction necessarily should have a large audience any more than good poetry has, and this doesn't mean it doesn't have a right to exist. Maybe minority writers are what we're talking about. How many serious readers of fiction are there in the country? Who knows, anyway, but there are not that many. I mean, we're really a country of a kind of mass quasi-literacy. We send people to college to teach them how to read things that take no intelligence to read.

The Fiction Collective, which I've been involved in, started out of this very situation. There are a number of good writers around who are not getting their books published or are getting them published in the imaginary way that Peter Davison talked about. The books were brought out very generously by the publisher with a small advance, occasionally got some very good reviews— even space reviews—and I've heard stories from some of the editors on this panel about books even reviewed on the first page or the third page of the *Times* that sold no more than twelve hundred or fifteen hundred copies. Hardback books are very expensive now; paper is expensive. Maybe serious readers don't want to put out ten dollars, twelve dollars for a book. It's a genuine problem, it seems to me, and there's no reason why publishers should necessarily be philanthropic, but I'd really like to have the reality out on the table. I've heard publishers and editors say for years now that all good fiction is published, and it's simply not so. You know, you begin to see this writer of ninety-five getting this letter of acceptance. He's had this manuscript circulating for fifty-five years. He dies happy.

Even if this were so—and I know it's not—I think it's a great burden on a writer to wait a number of years to have a book accepted. I think it slows down his production, it really changes him as a writer, and, consequently, I think it changes our literature. I don't know what the solution is. The Fiction Collective, which is a writers' cooperative, is a solution in a very small way. I think unless there are maybe a hundred fiction collectives operating in America or fiction is subsidized—perhaps the way the opera is, which may be a real solution—the problem's going to remain with us. I see no special reason why publishers should be more philanthropic than they are. And also, it seems to me a very real problem for the life of the country—the inner life of the country, the life of the imagination—that books that can't sell over five thousand copies or even over three thousand copies, which is by and large what Fiction Collective books have been selling—between twenty-five hundred and four thousand copies—that such books can't survive, can't find a publisher.

Davison:

Thank you, Mr. Baumbach.
Now, Mr. Laughlin of New Directions will speak to the point, or perhaps not.

James Laughlin:

I am very happy to be here. I think that Peter said it, about all. I don't know really what I can add. I advised my indulgent relatives not to attend this morning. I said it's going to be a day of deploring, and I think we must all very seriously deplore and then begin to try to invent some solutions, some of which may have to be very drastic. The gentleman on my left has made a very valiant beginning. I would say that, probably, however, if there were a hundred fiction collectives, there would not be enough readers to absorb all the product. That would be my only reservation to that. I think, perhaps, we should have five or ten fiction collectives, if they can begin to maintain anywhere near the standard which he has maintained.

I'd like principally to gasp a little bit about poetry publishing, because that's what I've been most closely involved with. We do try to publish a few novels but, perhaps with one or two exceptions, with a singular lack of success. I would like to talk more about poetry publishing, and I'd like to talk about time lag in poetry publishing, because it is not entirely true what Peter said, that you can't make money publishing poetry. You can make money if you are lucky, and if you wait long enough. You see, I was very, very lucky because I had the very good fortune to begin publishing at the time just after the last depression when nobody would touch poetry, and I fell heir—quite through no merit of my own but purely by happenstance—to great poets, such as Ezra Pound and William Carlos Williams, who were practically without publishers, and they in turn led me on to other great poets, such as Dylan Thomas, Tennessee Williams, Kenneth Rexroth, and then later, *Eros* people. Well, one shouldn't mention the names because one loves all equally. But the point is that in the life of a book of poetry, the first ten years are glum—they're just disastrous. People say, "Oh, it must be all those libraries that are buying poetry." Well, they aren't. I remember going once to the catalog of the library of the city of San Francisco and finding listed in the catalog the books of, I think, Robert Frost and three other poets as I went down my mental list of who were the good poets of the day. I don't imagine, really, that there are more than perhaps five hundred libraries which really buy poetry in a systematic and an extensive way.

So how, then, do you make money publishing poetry? You make it from the anthologists, the college professors putting together books to be used by their classes and classes in other schools and colleges that are required to pay a fee to the publisher which he splits with the poet. And you make it when the poet becomes well known enough so that his books—particularly his paperbacks—are assigned by professors in classes. And that's where the time lag comes in, because it's been my experience that if you publish a very good young poet, it's about, roughly, five to eight years before the anthologists begin to write in asking to reprint his poems in their anthologies and start paying you fees for that. And the time lag, until he gets good enough and famous enough so that a professor will actually put his book on the list for a contemporary poetry course, may be anywhere from ten to twenty years. In other words, what do you do while you wait? I think that is the question: What do you do while you wait? Now, in the case of New Directions, the loss on the new poet is made up from the profit on the established poets, may God rest their souls. Bill Williams and Ezra Pound and Dylan Thomas are paying annually at New Directions for the publication of three or four or five new and unprofitable poets who eventually—let us hope—will then pay, through their anthology fees and their college youth, for succeeding generations. In other words, it's a kind of rotating subsidy.

But there is this problem of a time lag, which produces a problem of working capital, which brings us to the subject of bank rates, which brings us to the subject of Ezra Pound's economics, which I will pass over. But let me say the old boy knew what he was talking about. He said, "Jas, don't ever get in the hands of the banks."

Now, there's one very practical matter that I'd like to touch on. Write to your congressman. As you know, revision of the copyright law has been under way for seven years. They've been tinkering with it over there for seven years, and the bill is coming up on the floor quite soon now, in the next few weeks, and it is terribly important that the provisions against unlimited Xerox or other copying not be watered down. This is terribly important for the future of all poets. This is terribly important for the continuation of the publishing of poetry by publishers. Now, it is perfectly obvious that if there is an obscure book, it is morally all right for a librarian to make a copy for a scholar in New Zealand who can't go out and buy the book. But if you have a situation, as you do now in so many colleges, where a professor is allowed to go down to the basement or hand the book to a secretary and say, "I'd like to talk a little bit about X tomorrow in my poetry course, and he isn't in the particular anthology which I am using, and of course I don't want the students to have to pay for his book, so will you please run me off thirty copies of these three poems by X?" Well now, I ask you, can you work it that way with your carpenter or your painter? Is this moral? Is this proper? And yet there is a very strong educational lobby from the people who should be our best friends, the college professors over there on the Hill, trying to get this copyright bill watered down so that multiple copying will be permitted. And if this happens, it will be a very, very serious blow to poets and to writers. So I strongly urge you to rush right home and find out who your congressman and your senator is—if like myself, a little vague, you don't always know—and urge him to vote for the copyright act—the revision of the copyright act as revised and as reported by the committee without weakening amendments. I think this is enormously important.

Davison:

I wish you were on the hustings in various states where they have congressmen, as opposed to the District of Columbia, so that you could press this. Still, here we are.

Next we'll hear from Frances McCullough of Harper & Row.

Frances McCullough:

Peter, first I'd like to disagree with you about cookbooks outselling novels. I think *Ragtime* is going to murder Julia Child this time around, and it is curious, though, that publishers are much more willing to invest money in a book like "Everything You Need to Know About Concrete" or a cookbook which is a sizable investment on the part of the company, which will sell maybe twenty-two hundred copies and disappear from the list, than they are to invest in serious novels or poetry. But I think what we're talking about here is a very complex situation. One part of it is that we have in about the past twenty years a terrific emphasis on education, on creative writing workshops, fellowships, creative writing colonies, and so on, that has produced a generation of really skilled writers. When I was first working in publishing in the early sixties, if we saw something that was good, we'd all jump up and down and say, "This guy can really write, this is really good," and we'd consider publishing it simply because the writing was good. That is now a given, that the writing is good. The general level of the craft is so far up that there is what Jon Baumbach talks about—a huge floating mass of good fiction that is not getting published.

On the other hand, lots of this emphasis has been more or less narcissistic, urging a kind of self-expression. It's produced a generation of writers, but it hasn't produced a generation of readers. In fact, it seems to have produced the opposite. In the sixties, college textbooks were aimed at eleventh-, twelfth-grade reading levels. Now they're aimed at ninth- and tenth-grade reading levels. If everyone who is now or ever was an English major bought one literary novel every year, we would all be in fantastic business. I can swear to you that there are more writers than readers. I know this to be true because I see their books. The majority of college kids read fad books, if they read at all. They don't have access to much else, with the exception of poetry. Sometimes the poetry-reading circuit generates a certain amount of access to writers, but poetry readings are already predigested to some extent, they're interpreted, and that really doesn't lead people back to books.

Publishers also have been increasingly relying on subsidiary rights income, which is largely closed to serious fiction and poetry. The actual bookstore sale, as people have been saying, discounting libraries and other institutional markets, is really appalling. One of our sales managers showed me a blow-by-blow sales description of a book that was very well reviewed and was known to everyone who knew what was going on, and there were less than two copies per state of actual books in the store, which was pretty horrifying.

Even for novels that have strong sales of, say, five to ten thousand—that's strong for us, I guess not strong for Doubleday—there is usually not a paperback offer. If these books don't or can't go into paperback, they're effectively dead. With the new hardcover prices at $10.00 or $12.50 for a chunky novel, they may be dead to begin with.

So, we have good writing, much of it unpublished, for what appears to be a very tiny market. It seems to me the central questions are: What is the market? How big is it? Who are they? How do you find them? The market is possibly dwindling and in all probability cannot afford to buy new books since they do not go into paperback. I'm very interested myself in treating serious literary fiction as I do poetry. I publish simultaneously in paperback hoping that at least there's a chance that the people who really want to read this book will be able to get it and will be able to tell other people about it. I think we need to explore mail-order distribution systems—all sorts of things that we have not sufficiently explored.

I also think that one of the central problems is not that you don't make money on these books, but every now and then you do; every now and then you have a fantastic success with a book that seems exclusively literary, and that, for many of us in publishing, is about the most exciting thing that can happen, and none of us are willing to let go of it. And that's also true for most authors. The chance at the big sale, at the big time, is really irresistible, and I think for that reason the small presses, the alternative presses, the collectives, and so on, can only go part of the distance.

Davison:

Thank you. Next is Diane Matthews of Doubleday.

Diane Matthews:

I hate to reiterate too much of what's been said before, but I do think there is a calculated risk involved in publishing serious fiction. There is always that chance that there'll be a major paperback sale or major awards. We have far more of a problem with poetry. As we all know, great poets need great audiences, and it just doesn't seem to be happening. With our normal collections, which we have been publishing both in hardbound and in paper, we sell an average of two thousand copies. At that rate of sale, to be technical, we're losing between $10,000 and $15,000 for every collection we publish. We have been forced to cut back on our list to minimize our losses, and thus we were less likely to take on young writers. We want people who have already established their audiences.

I think that another problem that we're meeting, aside from the delayed reaction to poets and working with a poet through his career—for instance, Roethke, whose collected work now will sell fifty thousand copies—is that the reviews are so delayed, and the review attention is so negative. The most outstanding one in the recent past is Helen Vendler's omnibus review in the *Times*. That did a tremendous disservice for poetry and for all of us who are working hard to get good poetry out.

We have, as I said, been forced to cut back on our list, and we publish an average of seven to ten books a year, plus anthologies, and we can't sign up more than four new poets a year, which I think is distressing. But we feel a responsibility to keep poetry, and because we are a large commercial house, we can take those losses—and I hope we continue to do so. But I think we do have to find the audience and to reach it. I feel so many people read the work of young poets in magazines and journals, but not many people are inclined to invest in the corpus of a person's work, and there has to be some way to reach the audience. Thank you.

Davison:

And now, Richard Seaver of Richard Seaver Books, the Viking Press.

Richard Seaver:

I was introduced as being from the Viking Press, and indeed I am, but our arrangement is perhaps one attempt to deal with the problem we are here for. We have what amounts to an independent publishing venture with our own catalog and editorial independence within the confines of the Viking Press. The Viking Press does all the hard work—that is, selling, warehousing, shipping, collecting money, and dealing with those banks from which one cannot get away. On the other hand, it enables us to concentrate, for better or for worse, on matters editorial, without being oblivious to business concerns. Nobody can be totally oblivious to the economics of book publishing, but at least we can concentrate our efforts on trying to publish the few books that we do each year on a personal-taste basis.

Of this present list of ours—I just did a quick rundown—we've heard that 10 percent of the total number of books published this past year was fiction. We have twenty books in this catalog—which is too many, already, for us—but eleven of those are fiction, two are volumes of poetry, and seven are nonfiction of a nature, such as almost to qualify them for fiction. They are either rather esoteric or difficult books, with one or two exceptions. Only one of those is a first novel, but four or five of those are second novels of which we have published the first, which, if anything, is worse than being a first novel. It's like bigamy: you've made the same mistake twice.

Betty Prashker mentioned that ten thousand copies was sort of the break-even point, at least for Doubleday. If that was our break-even point, not one of these books would have been published. Unfortunately, even though ours is lower, it's far too high, and I still maintain that a publisher's first obligation is to stay in business. Now, the delicate line you have to draw is how not to lose perspective. There is an article in the *Times* today which deals with tie-ins, and it all has to do with how to make a million dollars off one book quickly. I have a feeling that the pressures— especially economic—in book publishing are all in that direction, and the attempts to withstand them are more and more difficult. I perceive that in not very many years there will be no such thing as hardback publishing. I cannot conceive of our continuing in the direction we're going and publishing the books that we're publishing and the books that Mr. Laughlin and many others are publishing—in which we really have the greatest pride—and people going out and buying them for ten, twelve, and fifteen dollars. Somehow, we've got to bring costs down. One of the members of another of your panels, with whom I was talking earlier today, talked about a book which we had been involved with ten or twelve years ago—he as publisher, I as a book club editor at that point. We used it in the club. He wants to reissue it in paperback. It will cost as much today in paperback as it did in cloth ten years ago. If it were in cloth today, it would sell at double the original price. It was tough to sell then, it may be impossible to sell now.

I want simply to say that, in my own experience, I think the independent book publisher has to make a commitment to fiction and to poetry which cannot be token. Otherwise, it seems to me one of our basic functions. If we're in the book business, it's not for the money. Our basic thrust and purpose has been eliminated. And I'm also very concerned and leery of the rationale that we publish some commercial fiction to pay for the noncommercial fiction. I'm not talking about Mr. Laughlin here, who is an exemplary publisher in all respects, in my opinion, and who, indeed, over the decades has continued to keep that focus and has been rewarded for it. God help those who don't believe that there is virtue at the end of a commitment like that and whose poets are, indeed, after ten or twenty years, paying for the new ones he is publishing. What concerns me is the rationale that I'll just take on this commercial novel even though it really is shlock because it will help me pay for the poets and the first novelists I'd love to do but can't. What happens is, if indeed it's a success, you look for more schlock. And I have seen it. It's tough to resist when the banks are breathing down your neck.

I think it's time for me to stop.

Davison:

The last time I stood up here I was feeling very naked, since I was having to air my griefs and grievances first. I'm feeling much more reassured now, because I really haven't heard anything that seems to me to contradict what I said at the beginning. I don't feel any more encouraged or any more discouraged than I did. I would like to clarify one or two things and then ask for questions from the floor.

First, I think the point has been well made that there is a distinction between what is, in my terminology, the real business and the imaginary business of publishing. Imaginary business is why we're in it. The real business is what takes us to the banks.

Second, one best-seller does not a summer make. The point I was trying to make was that a book doesn't get singled out for this

vast audience unless it becomes a media event, unless somehow
or other the media take it up, unless somehow or other it ends up
widely reviewed in large media, on television, and the rest of it.
And that applies just as much to *Humboldt's Gift* and *Ragtime* as
to Hannah Green's excellent novel *The Dead of the House,* which
I was interested in twenty years ago. Doubleday was fortunate
enough to publish it.

Now, in view of the various comments that have been made and
the various angles of vision that have been taken, we'll be open to
questions from the floor. Please try to direct your question to one
person in particular. If you think you can be heard from where
you sit, ask me the question and I'll try to rephrase it. If you have
something a little lengthier you want to state, come down and talk
at the microphone here.

Audience:

I think that it would be nice if we knew exactly where we stood,
and ask each member of the panel to tell us what works of poetry,
what poets, and what good fiction they personally stand on—what
their publishers are faced with. I realize this is a good deal easier
with Mr. Zimmer, who has two books of poetry, than it is for Mr.
Laughlin, with his thirty or forty poets—we know who Jay publishes. But don't you think that would be a useful thing to know?
Who do you stand on? Who do you really like?

Davison:

The question is, Who do we stand on. All right, I'll begin while
others prepare their lists. I'm speaking of very recent works of
fiction and poetry. In poetry, Stanley Kunitz's work, David Igna-
tow's work, some of the work of James Tate; and in fiction, work
by David Wagoner, by John Sales whom most of you may not
have heard of, but who is a very fine writer, Ward Just, and Mat-
thew Vaughan, an English writer whom nobody's heard of, alas
and alack.

Audience:

Will you also give us sales figures? That's the crux of it.

Davison:

Well, I won't go into individual sales figures, but I mention it
regionally, however, because it seems to me a private matter between me and the author. I don't think Stanley Kunitz's sales
figures are your business, but I will say that not a single one of
those books—any of those books by any of those writers—has sold

over ten thousand copies.

Where shall we start here? Who's going to 'fess up first? Betty.

Prashker:

Well, let's see, do you want my schlock list? Or, first of all, let me say I don't have a schlock list. I think every book that I take on personally is a book of value. Some of them become best-sellers, but not because they're schlock. I would say one of the writers I admire very much is Marge Piercy. I published two novels of hers, and Diane published her book of poetry, *To Be of Use*. I think she's a marvelous writer. Now, *To Be of Use* is one of our best-selling poetry books, isn't it, Diane? How many copies have we sold?

Matthews:

About eight thousand in paper and fifteen hundred hard.

Prashker:

We've sold fifteen hundred hardcover and eight thousand in paper, and we're still not making money on that, at all. What is our minus figure on that?

Matthews:

I can't recall.

Prashker:

Well, we have a loss on that book so far. But, as Mr. Laughlin pointed out, we may get permission fees and I think the book will continue to sell in paperback.

Now, the novel is a good example of a book I consider a marvelous book. For one of the novels that I thought was really going to reach out into a large audience, there was a very disappointing performance on the part of the novel and a very disappointing performance, I thought, in the reception of the book by the reviewers. It got bad reviews. I won't go so far as to say it was badly reviewed, although I think it was. But here is an example of a publisher taking on both the fiction and the nonfiction and trying to make them go.

Now, there's another writer we published—John Leonard. He used to be the editor in chief of the *New York Times Book Review*. We published two of his novels, none of which have sold more than five thousand copies, and one of which was a candidate for the National Book Award. We published a book by Joy Williams called *State of Grace,* another candidate for the National

Book Award. It sold three thousand copies—absolutely fabulous book—and it was advertised, and it was well reviewed, but the natural audience never came out to buy it.

Davison:

Excuse me, could we move a little faster on our lists of books? Otherwise this question will never get answered, and we'll never get on to another one.

Baumbach:

Well, the Fiction Collective isn't really a publisher, but a writers' cooperative. But I'll mention our writers. Clarence Major, Mimi Albert, and Jerry Bumpus are in the latest list. Our list before was Ronald Sukenick, Mark Merrill, and Russell Banks; and our first list of authors was Peter Spielberg, B. H. Friedman, and Jonathan Baumbach.

Laughlin:

I love them all alike. I never try to pick out favorites because I wouldn't have published any one of them if I didn't like them, and I never give their sales figures because I think that's their business. I'll be glad to send you a catalog.

McCullough:

Sylvia Plath, Ted Hughes, Robert Bly, Russell Edson—whom I share with Jay a bit. Some lesser known: Yehuda Amichai, an Israeli poet; Gregory Orr, a young poet; Kathleen Fraser; Margaret Atwood; N. Scott Momaday; Paul West.

Matthews:

Josephine Jacobsen and Albert Goldbarth—both of whom were nominated for an NBA last year—Marge Piercy, Peter Wild, Michael Harper, Diane Wakoski, and Caroline Rogers, a young poet. And in fiction, I'm working with Joy Williams on a new novel and Margaret Craven, who turned out to be a media event, a seventy-five-year-old first novelist.

Seaver:

Being so small, it's, as with Jay, difficult for us to say which of our children we prefer, although having twenty children a year is somewhat of a problem. But we do publish William Eastlake; John Berger; William Burroughs; Juan Goytisolo, the Spanish writer; Octavio Paz, whom we share with Mr. Laughlin; and Richard

Gardner. Sales figures, again, I won't give you. I've told them
what they haven't sold more than.

Audience:

Is Octavio Paz the other poet besides Eastlake?

Seaver:

Paz and a poet named Barbara Guest. The two books we've just
brought out are both anthologies, but they are original anthologies: one, *The Negritude Poets,* the editor of which I believe is in
this room, Ellen Conroy Kennedy; and the second, published last
month, is a collection of native American poetry, mostly by young
people in their twenties.

Davison:

I hope that's sufficient existential self-definition. Do we have
other questions? Here.

Audience:

I get the impression that the best way to get poems published
would be to go home and write a lovely lyric poem about Judy
Garland or Watergate or sharks or something like that, in that
order. Do you really have to have all that much schlock?

Davison:

The question is, Is the best way to get a lyric poem published to
go home and write a poem about Judy Garland, Watergate, and a
shark, all in that order? Is that the best way to get a poem published? Is that question directed to anyone in particular?

Audience:

It's directed to the whole panel. Do you have to have some
gimmick?

Prashker:

The thing to do is to begin with the shark.

Audience:

Pardon?

Prashker:

Begin with the shark. Send it to the publisher. That's a good
way to begin—with the shark.

Audience:

It's not. He has pearly teeth.

Davison:

Question. Yes, back there. Yes, come down. This is David Godine, a publisher not on the panel.

David Godine:

I apologize, because I have three things to say, and it's going to take a little time.

First of all, Peter started with statistics, or Stanley did, and those are a little misleading because to be listed in the AAP or in Bowker you have to pay about $800 to $900 a year to belong to AAP, and this is something which is well beyond the means of small publishers. We just could afford it this year. Anyone who has been on the West Coast and seen the activity there or just seen what small presses are doing, I think, has to be convinced that there is a lot more activity, particularly in poetry, than is immediately evident from the AAP statistics. I think they're misleading. That's a very small point.

My second point is that if you do go by statistics and if you look at the statistics from 1920 to 1970, the horrifying thing is that the statistics, relative to the list, relative to the population, relative to the number of poets being published, are exactly the same today as they were in 1920. The only things that have changed are the prices, and the average price for poetry has gone from $3.82 to about $7 and some cents, not a substantial increase when you think of the increase in food. In other words, just as many books, proportionately, and almost absolutely, today are being published. And what's even worse, the horrifying thing which leads me to my last point, is that just as many are being sold. You look at Harcourt's list in 1923, you look at Liveright's list, you look at Knopf's list, when the figures are available, and you compare them to what is selling today, and you will find that the average is still, for a major poet, between two thousand and five thousand copies. And this is with the population of the country going from approximately 110 million people to 200 million people. So the real key—and this is something that only Fran McCullough touched on—is the market out there. If Doubleday, the greatest merchandising and marketing machine in this country—I mean they are the Sears, Roebuck of publishing—can only sell ten thousand copies, and they consider that break-even, my mind boggles at how few of the 200 million people in this country are buying books. And if that's for novels, the statistic for poetry is absolutely appalling.

Now, the conclusion I draw from this is twofold, and you have to compare America to the rest of the world. When a new book of poetry is published in Russia, it's a half a million copies for the first printing—doesn't matter who it is. A poet reads, and you couldn't buy seats in Madison Square Garden in Russia, and that's true of eastern Europe. There aren't that many people in this country reading poetry. They're buying poetry, and I'm reminded here of Kenneth Patchen's great comment: "People who say they love poetry and don't buy any are a bunch of cheap sons-of-bitches." It's a great quote, and a lot of people in this country say they really love the stuff, and boy, they'll do anything for it. But when you ask them when was the last time you plunked $3.95 down for a softcover book: "Uh, uh, I go to the library or I get it from Xerox." So, the first key conclusion is, because publishers are not stupid—Doubleday is not stupid—if there were a market out there for poetry, if people were buying it, if Doubleday could market it, they would be publishing it. Now, nobody goes to Ford Motor Company and screams at Ford for discontinuing the Edsel, and I don't think it's fair to go to Doubleday or any trade house and scream at them for being low in poetry. People are not buying it.

That's number one. And the second thing that nobody's touched on, which I think really has to be said, is that the distribution of books in this country is archaic. It is abominable; it is absolutely absurd. I don't know how many of you people know how books are distributed, but if you're in the business, and you ever describe how they're distributed to someone who's in a real business, a look of blank confusion—if not terror—comes over their faces and they say: "That's not a business. Are you kidding yourself? You can't be serious." Try it sometime. And until the Doubledays and the Vikings and the Random Houses and the McGraw-Hills and the Macmillans get together among themselves and say, "This is archaic. If we have to sell ten thousand copies of a book to break even, there's something wrong," there's really something wrong. And until they get together—cooperatively, as an assocation—and they work this, then it's never going to be any better for people like Jay Laughlin, myself, or any other small publisher. They've got to take the initiative here. That's all I have to say.

Davison:

Thank you. As a footnote to these remarks, I fear I must mention two things. One is the Federal Trade Commission and the Antitrust Act—but not as a matter of defense, simply as a matter of an additional part of the scenery. Second, I think it is wonderful about the size of printings of poetry in Russia, but it is a trifle selective and does not include Osip Mandelstam, and for a great long time it did not include Anna Akhmatova. So there are differences.

Next question. Yes, ma'am.

Audience:

A number of reasons have been given for the fact that books do not sell, that there's a dearth of readers, and I'm afraid I, in my humble opinion, want to say something which is very pessimistic. I think it's going to get worse, and my reason is this: in the schools they are not cultivating taste—no appreciation for quality. I'll give you one example. One of my ten grandchildren, in the seventh grade, was given a reading list. Nothing of the great books, nothing of the classics, nothing of good literature today—you can use the term, if you want to, *schlock.* A book for a seventh-grader about a young black girl who had to choose between an abortion or having an illegitimate child. Surely there's something more. This can be discussed in sociology or whatever. But to have this in a list for book review for a seventh-grader when there is a lot of good literature?

Davison:

Did everybody hear the question? Next, sir.

Audience:

A great many people in the publishing business are people whose hearts and minds are pure and who have the respect for perfection that publishers once had for authors, but who face a hard, cruel world in which there is mammon out there and mighty little of God. Incidentally, I'm in the professoring business, so the most profitable writing I have done over a long career is a couple of hundred dollars worth of excessive words for some encyclopedia pieces. The professional stuff you write you're glad to see published anyway, because you feel you have that drive and compulsion to share with other people things that are interesting. I'd like to suggest that Mr. Laughlin doesn't know about the copyright business. That maybe that point of view is wrong. Maybe the ten to twenty years that it takes to get some return on new poets, through their use in anthologies and classrooms and what not, will be accelerated by allowing the Xerox of thirty copies instead of holding out for an insignificant alleged royalty anyway, and accelerated to the point where even poets will be able to come out of their garrets and sing on the streets.

Davison:

I think Mr. Laughlin's point was that there is no remuneration for such photocopying. The author gets nothing for it.

Audience:

I was thinking about the publicity end of it.

Davison:

Well, it's a subject which I'm sure will be discussed, especially at the fourth panel tomorrow. Was there a question? Is there an answer you'd like to give?

Laughlin:

I would like to hope that you were right, but if you look at the arithmetic, the number of schools and colleges, and assume that each teacher of English is permitted to Xerox multiple copies for his classes, I can see nothing but disaster, simply from the fact that anthologies will become obsolete. Each professor would then make his own anthology on the Xerox machine, and the prescription of paperbacks for use in courses would fall away to four or five major figures in a contemporary poetry course, and your ten or twelve B-plus people will simply be done by Xerox.

Audience:

My point is that I think that kind of use is comparable to the copying of short passages for purposes of review with appropriate credit. It's advertising. It's developing a taste for the author that's ultimately—

Davison:

But sir, the point is that if the author's taste is developed to that point, there will be no copies of the author's work for anybody to buy. I'm sorry to be contentious about this. I think we should change the subject. Ma'am, back there.

Audience:

May I offer a slight comfort to, at least, in my experience, being asked not to use the Xerox machines. The meanings have been squeezed and invariably altered, and it's not like having your assignment sheets Xeroxed. May I ask a naive question?

Davison:

To whom is it addressed, please, if you could address it to somebody?

Audience:

Let's say Mr. Laughlin. I know more about his list than I do about the others. Why can't we put out paperbacks? I'd like to pose a naive question and forget about hardbacks, except for things like the collected works of Shakespeare or something that we think people may actually buy and plunk down money for. Why can't we just do paperbacks?

Laughlin:

Well, I think there are two answers to that question. First, the libraries that do buy poetry books want clothbound books that stand up under the punishment of use, if they are used. And, you know, really, if you look into the accounting of the production department, you'll find that the actual cost difference between doing the paperback and doing the clothbound really only boils down—if you look at the unit—to a difference, perhaps, of forty cents in the binding cost and whatever you pay for the jacket, which might be a total of around eighty cents altogether. So that what you're really talking about is the number of copies which you guess you can print. You see, your substantial basic costs are in composition—which is now very high—in paper, in press run, in the binding operation, the sewing and covering operation. The way publishers now, as far as I know, allocate their costs is that they go through a kind of mystic procedure where they say, "We're going to do one thousand copies hardbound for libraries, and we will allocate so much of cost to this, and then we will risk doing, say, three or four thousand copies in paperback, and we will allocate so much of cost to that."

The only real way, substantially, to get your prices back to where you would like to have them, to where they were two, three, five years ago, would be if you could be confident that, with a new poet, you could print, say, seventy-five hundred copies. Then you could get the cost of books down.

McCullough:

I might add that we are publishing all our poetry in paperback now, and the problem with that is that the royalty rates are lower for the author.

Davison:

The book is published at $2.95, with the author's royalties about 30¢ a copy.

McCullough:

Could I answer that too? I had that same idea a few years ago, and I thought I was being very clever by publishing two poets only in paperback. One was Louis Simpson, who I was sure would get reviewed. They didn't. There are so many books being published that anything that gives reviewers an excuse not to review a book, they will take. Neither of the books got reviewed. The other thing that happened was that in the bookstores they were not put out with new books. They were stuck off in the corner of the paperback section upstairs. They were not considered new books—they were not considered books, in fact.

Laughlin:

That's quite true. I would bear that out in both cases. Very few media review paperbacks unless they are also clothbound.

Davison:

First, Mr. Eshleman, and then Mrs. Williams.

Clayton Eshleman:

I'd like to address this to anyone on the panel who would like to respond. I'm working in the Poetry-in-the-Schools program in Los Angeles right now; I work with seventh-, eighth-, and ninth-graders. One of the toughest things for me to deal with is a real, in general, negative attitude towards reading that seems to be firmly ingrained in most of the students. And I have students that are referred to as mentally gifted minors—they are select students. So it seems to me that something happens to people between the time that they first learn to read and the time that they become seventh-graders, which creates a small problem. I don't even really know how to ask this question. It seems to me that the real thing is education, and what can be done about that? Because when you have people that are turned off, I mean, most of the students think it's really dumb that I bother to write poetry in the first place. This is an attitude that they hit me with when I come into the classroom. So if you have people who are turned off at that point, then of course the situation is going to be like it is. So what do we do about that? Is there a connection—

Davison:

Can people in the back hear this question? No. I'll summarize it in a minute. Go on.

Eshleman:

Is there a vital connection in any sense between publishing and education?

Davison:

Well, the question is: Mr. Eshleman teaches in courses in schools in Los Angeles, and a great many of the students who are supposed to be specially gifted don't read—are not interested in reading. Is there any direct connection between publishing and education? The answer is that the largest amount of money taken in by the publishing business in this country is for textbook publishing, but if you're limiting yourself to trade publishing, yes, there is. And I would rather let the house representatives of publishers who deal much more with educational publishing take this question, if there be any here. By golly, there's not a one. Betty, speak.

Prashker:

Peter, I think that the question really hits the heart of the matter, and I don't think it has anything to do with educational publishing. I think it has to do with the fact that kids really not only think it's dumb to write poetry, they think it's dumb to read poetry, and they think it's dumb to read anything. And I think part of it is that they are assaulted by all other kinds of media all the time, such as television, movies, and so forth. The idea of curling up with a good book is somehow foreign to them. It seems to me that if we here are serious about our wish to get a wider audience for poetry and serious fiction, then we must reach down to that level and try to get kids enthusiastic about reading. Absolutely.

Baumbach:

Can I say something, Peter? In my other life I'm on the board of directors of something called the Teachers' and Writers' Collaborative, which is involved in this very problem, and I think what we run into all over the country are teachers who teach poetry who really dislike it and present it like a kind of medicine, and, after a point, you'd just rather be sick. So, what's been happening, and I think it's very important, is that writers are going into schools—going into grade schools, poets and fiction writers—

and sort of presenting themselves and their work in a wholly different way. Again, it's one of these battles that may take three or four lifetimes, which I am afraid none of us have.

Davison:

We may never catch up. Galen, you had a question?

Galen Williams:

I had a question for Fran McCullough. If you were given all the money in the world to find an audience, where would you begin?

McCullough:

Well, I think the first place I would go is college campuses. And when I was discussing the question of the audience, my deep suspicion is that they don't exist.

Williams:

Even with the money.

McCullough:

Even, I think, if you had the money, you would probably find that this is a deep cultural problem that goes right across the board, that is so serious that we have trouble talking about it. I think that, well, on a practical level, one thing I would do is try to pick up on some of the things that the small presses have been doing. I think that there is a lot of room for exchange between the big publishers and the small publishers and the way that we approach our markets. They need to know more about getting into the bookstores, and we need to know more about mail order and the various ways that they've been able to approach people. That's not really a very serious answer. I would have to think about it for a while.

Davison:

I think that we are talking, on this particular panel, about what is supposed to be a real business. I tried in my opening remarks to say something of why I think, when dealing with poetry and serious fiction, there's something imaginary about the business we transact. There's nothing imaginary about publishing as such, and the subsequent panels that you're going to hear are dealing with people who are not in real business, in the sense that they are there for a profit. And that is another aspect of it. The largest question mark we have—and if anybody has a simple answer for it, he's probably cracked—is: Why can't you reach a real audience for serious literature through the most businesslike methods that this civilization has been able to develop?

Audience:

Well, I think that you did answer that question with words of total democracy in America. You told us that more than thirty years ago Americans were the best-educated people in the world and are the least concerned. Part of the reason is that you were always concerned with trade, making a buck, quick reactions, etc., and therefore you could not spend time with more serious, patient, intellectual endeavor. A publishing writer certainly needs to commit himself in our society to getting his work published. I don't think you'll see much patience for serious fiction as long as you're not on the television set. And a dedication to smashing that machine, on one level, would sell more books for you quicker than anything else.

The only other thing that I think is interesting, to pick up on a comment that one panelist made, is that there is an absolutely incredible number of voices of writers, and it's really hard to tell—there are so many more writers than readers—it's hard to build around them. You don't know whom to listen to, and it's very hard to know as a reader—a particular college student I'm speaking of—whom to be able to develop.

Davison:

So perhaps that's why we wait for the media to tell us. And that's why the books singled out by the media are the ones that sell over ten thousand copies. Yes, ma'am.

Audience:

The suggestion has been made that the audience doesn't exist. Ms. McCullough said that she suspected it would turn out to be true. And a suggestion was made at one point—I forget by which panelist—that poetry that's performed in poetry readings is in a sense mediated or predigested. I would like to suggest that that is the natural way of working with poetry, which was an oral art to start with, and that it is no accident that large audiences frequently do turn out, whether on college campuses or elsewhere, for poetry readings. It's no accident that some poets had the foresight to bring copies of their books along to their readings and peddle them, sell them. This is how we should be selling poetry in the first place.

I was also troubled by Miss Matthews's reference to Helen Vendler's mammoth reviews, which I don't like much because they do denigrate poetry in the sense of cramming many books into one small amount of space. But I remember the books that she particularly attacked, the inspirational verse. And I remember at least one letter to the *Times* which said that those books were being published not as poetry but as religious verse. Now I don't know whether that's in terms of the organization of a publishing house, whether that's so—I assume it is. But in terms of the market, in the bookstores, specifically in Doubleday bookstores that I went into, those books are on the poetry shelves, and there are damn few other poetry books on the poetry bookshelves.

Davison:

I should also make as a footnote to a fact involved there, that those books are sent to all poetry reviewers, since I am one and receive them. But there was a question, and I can't remember how it began or to whom it was addressed.

Audience:

I'm sorry. The answer, it was addressed to Miss Matthews, and I suppose part of the question that I left out was: How can the so-called schlock books that all of the publishers are publishing to finance the serious list do that job? How can your sales of inspirational verse plunge ahead of the sales of your serious verse, if the serious verse is not on the shelves in the bookstores?

Matthews:

That surprises me. I just know that the inspirational verse is not labeled as poetry. They're called prayers and conversations with God.

Prashker:

On the flat copy, it says that they're prayers.

Davison:

Somebody sent you the wrong list.

Baumbach:

You're an answer to those prayers.

Davison:

I think there was one. May I make a comment on that question? As a word for Helen Vendler: prior to her long reviews in the *New York Times*—which you may like or you may not—the *New York Times* was reviewing no contemporary poetry. It seems to me unquestionably an improvement, whether you differ in opinion or not. Next question. Sir, back there.

Audience:

Hello. I would like to make a few comments about the reason why people don't buy books these days. For five years I've carried out research on this particular issue. I've found out that most of the book publishers these days don't publish really beautiful books anymore. The only beautiful books that are being published today are the art books. Poetry is a very serious thing, and in the ancient days up to the early nineteenth century, poetry books were always printed with good graphic designs and so on. But these days they just throw the print on the paper. It's so dull, and it doesn't attract, you see. And poetry is very vital. I think the publishers have to change their attitudes toward the printing of poetry books, the design, the texture of the paper—all these things that count towards attracting people to buy these books. So I think that once we start to move on this level, the sales volume will increase.

Another thing is that media change. The attitude toward poetry has also changed. Now, poetry books are not retailed on the same level as novels in terms of publicity. They are not. Whenever a new novel is published, you see it on television, in the media, and so on, and then you also see the writer interviewed on television and the other media. But seldom will you see a great poet interviewed and given the same consideration as an author of fiction. Why does this happen? And obviously people are taught by TV and the news media, so I think we have to change the attitude toward poets, too, that they are also imaginative people and they also belong to the high level of intellectuals. So that's all I have to say.

Audience:

I'd like to go back to the earlier question of paperbacks versus hardbacks.

Davison:

Do you want to direct this to anyone in particular?

Audience:

No, because several members of the panel commented, I think there were about three answers given, all of which seemed to me quite unpersuasive. One was that it really only costs forty cents more to produce a hardcover book than a paperback. If that is so, when the hardcover books are being sold for twice as much, it seems to me that something needs to be explained there.

The second answer was if poets are put out in paperback, nobody would review them. Well, if the publishers started putting out all their poetry, say, in paperback, it seems to me they would be reviewed, obviously.

And further, we're told that the royalty to the author is only thirty cents on a paperback. Well, this is an arrangement. There are certain arrangements that exist. If they were all put out in paperback, I would think other arrangements could be made.

Since those three answers were given by three different people, I'd be interested to know if there is any further explanation.

Davison:

Yes, sir, there is, and I'm going to take that question myself. It took me a great many years in the publishing business to learn the answers to some of those questions, and it may not be possible for me to state them simply. I did, however, speak in my opening remarks about the economy of scale. It is obviously cheaper, if you printed 50,000 copies of a book, to print each of those copies than it is to print one copy of the book, because you have to set all the type no matter whether you're printing one copy or 50,-000. If you are printing 10,000 copies, it costs more to print each of those 10,000 copies than it does each of 50,000. The economy in doing paperbacks is eventually in the size of the printing, not in what it's bound in. Forty cents a copy is exactly right—it may be a little higher now, what with inflation—but putting the hard binding on it costs nothing. The principal problem is, how many people can you expect to distribute it to? Whether a book is paperback or hardcover depends on where it's going to go. If you're planning to put a copy of your book—five copies of your book— in every drugstore rack in the United States and begin by printing 300,000 copies, it's obvious it's going to be easier than if you print 3,000 copies of a chapbook of poetry. Now, if you went into this bookstore—this drugstore—with a new book of poetry in paperback, how many copies do you think would be on the drugstore rack at the end of the week when the salesman comes back to clean it out? All five copies. That would be nice if we could do it that way, but drugstores aren't in the business of selling poetry.

Second. If all publishers did their poetry in paperback, would it be reviewed? The answer to that question is very simple. Almost all publishers are doing almost all their poetry in paperback and almost all of it is not being reviewed.

The third answer to the question is about royalty. Yes, the poet or the fiction writer gets a percentage of the published price. That's his royalty; that is an arrangement, quite right. It's a historical arrangement; it's a fairly just arrangement. You can argue about the percentage that he should have, but 15 percent of a dollar is fifteen cents, 30 percent of a dollar is thirty cents. If you sell the book for a dollar, and you have to pay to print it, there's only so much you can take to pay the author, unless you believe that publishers should be subsidizing this or that the government should be subsidizing publishers, which I don't ask for. The fact is that we have not discussed very much arithmetic, and arithmetic is what governs a great many of these problems. Poets whom I publish and whose work I adore are stuck with the same problem. They want their books to be read and used in courses and in schools, and therefore they want the price to be low. But they also—since they're normal people and have to buy meals—would like to earn money from them. And the lower the price the less money you earn; the higher the price, the fewer copies you sell. This is the law of supply and demand. It operates in all sorts of odd ways, and the interaction between reviewing, printing, publishing, binding, and the quantity that goes out is very complicated. Now, I'm sure that that's an incoherent way of expressing it, but. . . . Anybody else want to speak to that, or have I hammered it into the ground?

Now, question. I think we only have time for one more question, I'm afraid. One more question.

Audience:

I have a question about poetry. Four years ago I stood in line for two hours to get into this place to hear some poetry read by Yevtushenko, and we had a line that went completely around the building—six deep. We certainly couldn't get in to hear him. But as was pointed out, there is a difference between the reading of poetry and the reading of poetry. It does have a relevance, I think, to the selling of publications. And this, of course, is through television, through the publicity you can gain through television. And now that we have—as was pointed out in the *New York Times* today—so many of our publishers owned by RCA and MCA and CBS and NBC Television, shouldn't there be some kind of an input from you people and from other people in publishing into these television programs, and present poets in the act

of reading poetry, and therefore have a kind of a one-to-one relationship between television and the publishing of poetry books?

Davison:

To whom is that question addressed?

Audience:

That's directed to the gentleman from the Atlantic Monthly
Press.

Davison:

To me. Well, the answer to the question is yes. Sure, we should.
It would be wonderful if we could. I think you'll find a lot of educational television does it, I think the Classic Theatre series that is
being done by Channel 2—

Audience:

I think it should be done by commercial television.

Davison:

Commercial television, why is that better?

Audience:

I think it's better because people, especially children, assume
that if it's good, it's going to be on commercial television. If it's
not good, it's not going to be on it.

Davison:

Well, they get an awful lot of jingles in the morning for cereals.
I think it would be wonderful if that happened. I think's it's un-
likely. Most of the poetry programs I hear on commercial television and radio—and when I was a child I used to perform on
them—are of the sort in which a lady moans some poetry for fifteen minutes and goes away. And I think that is highly counter-
productive.
    I think that I'd like to summarize what we've talked about today
by asking you the questions: How real is this business that you
have heard described here? How imaginary is it? How does one
connect the reality of business with the area of imagination on
which your imaginary forces work? Thank you.

Publication by University and Small Presses

Paul Zimmer, chairman; Daniel Halpern; Willard Lockwood; Dudley Randall; Jeri Sherwood; Jack Shoemaker; Mark Vinz

Kunitz:

We are ready to begin our second panel which will be a discussion by persons involved in university and small-press publishing. The chairman of the panel is Paul Zimmer, who has had a varied background in the publishing world and the bookselling world. He has been Macy's book department manager in San Francisco, he was manager of the San Francisco News Company, and manager of the UCLA bookstore. He is now associate director of the University of Pittsburgh Press and editor of the Pitt Poetry Series, one of the most adventurous, let me say, and valuable of all the poetry series being published.

To add to his virtues and accomplishments, he is a distinguished poet and has published several books of poems, has received the Borestone Mountain Award in 1971, and a National Endowment grant, in 1974, I believe. I'm glad to introduce Mr. Zimmer.

Paul Zimmer:

It's kind of unfair in some ways, I think, that this panel should be in the afternoon, after drinks and lunch, and so forth, because I don't think we'll be nearly as coherent as the morning panel. I'm going to stand up here and kind of erupt like a volcano. I think what we'll do is follow the same format that was followed this morning. I'll give a brief talk, introduction, and then members of the panel can make statements, and then I think we can open it to the floor.

I'd like to introduce the members of my panel. This is Daniel Halpern of Ecco Press on my left here. Willard Lockwood of Wesleyan University Press, Mrs. Arthur Sherwood from Princeton

39

University Press, Dudley Randall of Broadside Press, Jack Shoe-maker of the Sand Dollar Press, and Mark Vinz of Dacotah Territory Press.

In 1937 a very promising young poet named Theodore Roethke, whose work had been receiving some attention through his publications in literary magazines, received a letter from the publishing house of Macmillan, asking him whether he had a full manuscript ready to be considered for publication. Roethke was not prepared with a full book and sadly had to deny their request, but he did so with the confidence that when he was ready to publish a book, there would be a trade publisher interested in considering it.

Times have changed. I am certain that the people of this panel and many who are in the audience are aware of the increasing difficulties that poets and fiction writers are experiencing. In these dark, inflating, conglomerating, post-Nixon days, fine writers, and particularly new writers, are experiencing grave difficulties in having their work published. Even many of the venerable literary agents, the traditional purveyors of the "new" writer, have begun to charge healthy fees for simply considering the representation of a manuscript of an "unknown" writer. Most commercial publishers long ago discontinued the practice of considering manuscripts of poetry or fiction coming in "over the transom." In fact, many of them reply even to letters of inquiry with poorly duplicated forms of rejection. In articles and interviews in journals and trade magazines, they plead the excruciating difficulties of the financial squeeze. They claim also that pressures from their parent companies to publish only profitable books have forced them to forsake poetry and short-story collections. The problem has become brutally apparent to the poet and fiction writer. In fact, I feel we are here today to consider what must be termed a very real crisis for the arts of fiction and poetry writing in this country.

Though many commercial publishers claim that it is economically impossible for them to continue to pioneer new talent in poetry and fiction, I note how willingly they swoop down to snatch up a writer like James Dickey or Richard Brautigan from the small presses when the author has proven himself hot. I also note the many requests I receive from their text divisions, asking for permission to republish in classroom books the poems of the poets that we have had the wit and courage to publish originally. I am grateful for these requests, incidentally. It would seem that by their refusal to speculate on new talent they are neglecting a social responsibility similar to that which large industrial firms are now being forced to accept through larger degrees of pollution control. And just *who* can truly afford to test unknown talent through publication?

As the editor of one of the most active poetry lists in the country, I am increasingly aware of how much the burden has fallen to the small presses and the university presses. In the past few years the University of Pittsburgh Press, through the administration of the International Poetry Forum's United States Award, has annually considered between one thousand and sixteen hundred first manuscripts of poetry a year. Over the seven years of the existence of our poetry series, we have looked at a total of approximately nine thousand poetry manuscripts. In addition to this, each week I receive at least one or two letters of query from veteran poets—many of them refugees from the commercial publishers—who are seeking homes for their new work. We are able to publish an average of six poetry books a year. Up to midsummer of this year, we had published forty-four books of poetry during the existence of our series. This includes the contest winners, some translations sponsored by the International Poetry Forum, and over thirty books of our own selection. This is, I grant, a very healthy poetry publishing record, but I point out that what we publish is only one-half of one percent of all that we have considered. And we are forced to reject many manuscripts that we feel are eminently publishable.

Let me continue with some more dismal statistics. The most that any single title of poetry has sold in our series is 5,600 copies, and the least has been 400. The average sale of the book has been approximately 1,350 copies. Thus, in seven years we have sold almost 60,000 books of poetry. Sixty thousand is .02 percent of the number of people who will pay to see the Cincinnati Reds play baseball this year. Sixty thousand is .007 percent of all the people who have purchased a copy of *Jaws*. Sixty thousand—this is a total sale of all the poetry books we've ever done—is approximately .0003 percent of the total population of the United States. Not taking into consideration that some single customers buy many of our titles, this means that perhaps one person in 3,600 might buy a copy of one of our poetry books. Count up to 3,600 slowly if you wish to have some sense of the interest in poetry in this country. I do not have statistics on fine fiction, but I am reasonably certain the record is equally as difficult. Thus, the fine writer, as always, remains "alone with America."

I wish I could feel that the strong manuscripts we are forced to reject will be published elsewhere. I am not certain that this is the case. As I have said, basically the job of publishing poetry and short stories has fallen on the university presses and the small presses. There are the heroic efforts across the country of such excellent small publishers as Unicorn Press, Black Sparrow Press,

New Rivers Press, Jonathan Williams, David Godine, Kayak, Sand Dollar, Something Else Press, Dryad, Ithaca House, City Lights, Broadside Press, Barn Dream Press, Ecco Press, Territorial Press, October House, and Stone Wall Press, to name just a few. I wish I could name them all. University presses that offer traditionally excellent poetry publishing programs are Wesleyan, L.S.U., Yale, and, I modestly add, Pittsburgh. Then new programs and competitions for new poets and fiction writers have sprung up in the past years: for poetry, the University of Missouri's Devins Award, the Juniper Award of the University of Massachusetts Press, and modest new poetry publishing programs at Princeton, Georgia, and Virginia. Illinois, L.S.U., and Iowa have begun limited programs for the publication of short fiction.

These are notable efforts, most of them rising out of the concern for the plight of fine writing in this country. However, the situation remains troublesome. All of us have sadly witnessed the mortality rate of small presses over the years. It is a brave but financially debilitating business, and there are few people who can long afford this labor of love, especially in these days of the rampant economy. The other grim reality is that many university presses are experiencing serious financial trouble. They make few points with financial administrators for their efforts in publishing poetry and fiction, and several excellent scholarly presses—in fact, publishers of poetry—have been buried by their administrations in the past few years. Others have faced terrible crises and barely managed to squeak through on a modified basis. It is quite possible that in the next few years the ranks of the university presses will diminish further. Finally, just in case it is not apparent to this audience, practically all university presses operate at a deficit to their institutions.

What I am attempting to demonstrate with all of this is that the publication of fine writing in this country is being essentially left to a group of small but staunch publishers with what would appear to be limited means. The commercial publishers—though they may dabble a bit for prestige—are not risking the "big money" on untested talent or properties which might have a limited appeal. If commercial publishers continue their trend toward the publication of only safe commercial books and if more small presses and university presses begin to perish, where will the poet or fine fiction writer go? The prospects are grim.

Some foundations and private individuals, recognizing the crisis, have begun to make grants to the university presses and small presses. I can personally testify to the generosity of the National Endowment for the Arts in making grants for the publication of fine writing. There are other foundations, both local and national, that have shown a similar generous concern. But private foundations, I note in recent articles, are beginning to experience their own financial pinches.

The audience for poetry and fine fiction may be limited in this country, but basically it has always been served, even to some extent during the depression of the twenties and thirties, by the intelligent commercial publication of books. One wonders what is truly wrong now, when, in a nation of over 200 million people it may well be necessary for the government and a few benevolent private institutions to finance what can be salvaged of the best and most significant writing that is done in this country. My feeling is that what these worthy institutions do should be supplementary to fine publishing in this country, not the basis of what is done.

Let me assume the pulpit for just a few moments more and address the larger issue. This may be my only chance to cry hellfire where it may really matter. The problem—like the price of our groceries and everything else—lies with the economic conditions of the 1970s, which are now beginning to have their debilitating effect on our very culture, the excellence of our art, the fineness of our minds, and, therefore, the strength of our civilization. I am referring to the inflated prices, the windfall profits, and concentration of wealth and power which results in the conglomerations of big business—yes, I mean publishing conglomerations—the kind of big business that prevails over its subordinates to forsake its responsibility to qualify for what is merely profitable.

As I have shown, the fine writer has only a small piece of turf in this country, yet I know that all present here recognize the extreme importance of this holding. It is up to us, as publishers, to strive valiantly to continue to give him or her a place to go. That is the very important consideration of this panel and this two-day meeting. It is a serious responsibility, and we are the people who must, with or without help, strive to continue to offer the kind of encouragement and hope that only publication can give to an excellent writer.

Thank you.

I believe Daniel Halpern will begin by making a few remarks.

Daniel Halpern:

There's something slightly ironic about commercial publishers telling us that it costs $20,000 to produce a book of poems, but I know that you can produce a beautiful book of poetry for under $5,000. Granted, there is the overhead and the other problems that a large commercial publishing house has that a small press doesn't have. If these publishers are going to do four books of poetry per year at $80,000, I suggest that they might think about splitting that cost in half, find a method of distribution, printing, and production, and still publish ten books as opposed to four.

And this idea that we can't publish paperbacks seems to me ridiculous. I wanted to talk about that when somebody brought that point up this morning. If publishers got together and told the New York Times Book Review, in a certain way, or the New York Review of Books, to review paperback poetry, paperback poetry would be reviewed. After all, it's the same poetry that's in the hardcover edition, and the fact that it has cloth covers seems, in the end, to be rather insignificant. And who set up this policy of only reviewing hardcover editions to begin with? The reviewers or the publishers?

The talk this morning about paperback publishing being out isn't right. There are problems of initial plant costs, production costs, which the hardcover editions somehow take care of, but one could print a library edition so that it would still have one thousand, two thousand copies printed for the library sale.

Reviewing, though, is not really the issue—reviewing, that is, such as it is at the moment. But I don't want to talk too much about that. I really want to talk about something else, which is more positive.

I started the American Poetry Series at the Ecco Press in 1972, and since then we've done six collections—two a year. I think it's important to say that my situation is not really a typical one in that I was luckier than many small presses. I had a publisher who was interested in serious literature and trusted my taste. I also had a commercial press to distribute my books. That, too, was luck. Tom Guinzberg of the Viking Press happens to be a publisher who feels that poetry is important enough to counterbalance the loss these books incur. So I had the advantage of enough money to print books of poetry in what I hope is a handsome format, a national distributor, and no one to question what I wanted to publish. It seemed obvious that the best way to publish poetry was to create a series that would generate interest in and of itself, enough interest to carry those first books by poets unknown even to readers of poetry. I'm thinking of James Reiss or David McElroy. Well, the idea seems to have worked. The series has received its fair share of national review attention. The New York Times Book Review has reviewed all the books in the series. I don't know what was involved in that, but the books were reviewed.

In starting the Ecco series, I learned a great deal about the way publishing works. Since we don't have a publicity department or an advertising department or a subsidiary rights department, we do everything ourselves—that's two people. I was told early on, by people like Jay Laughlin and Tom Guinzberg, that it was word of mouth that sold books of poetry, novels, that sold books in general. That would make a good publishing motto, maybe. Anyway, it took me three years to figure out that the best way to get the word rolling was just to tell people about the books. Once I developed a list of two or three hundred interested people around the country, people who were in touch with other people, the sales began to pick up. Readers began ordering early volumes in the series when they saw them listed on the later books.

I suppose what impressed me most in dealing with commercial publishers was that they knew absolutely nothing about publishing poetry—and I don't mean that, it sounds pejorative, but I don't mean it in that way. And the fact that they lost money or lose money is primarily their own fault. Salesmen rarely spend too much time trying to sell that token book of poetry on a list, and obviously there are, you know, a good number of exceptions in New York. There are people working for commercial publishers who do care about poetry. The trouble is that they cannot have the power to implement that interest, but they are there. Diane Matthews, this morning, from Doubleday, Alice Quinn at Knopf, Alida Becker at Viking, and Pat Strong at Farrar, Straus are all people—and all women—who are interested in the publishing of poetry and who are constantly trying to get their publishers to do more poetry. And of course there is Harry Ford at Atheneum, who does have the power, and, consequently, they have one of the most prestigious lists of poetry in the country. The confusion the commercial publishers experience in putting out a book of poems comes not from an inability to figure things out. It isn't worth it to them to figure it out.

But I should be talking about small presses. Let it suffice to say that the commercial publishers are publishing poetry, yet there is a hell of a lot of poetry out there that is not being published. That's where we come in. Or, at least, where I believe Ecco comes in. I was told that all good books eventually find a publisher. We heard that this morning. In fact, I was told this last Friday when I called up two or three of the biggest publishers in New York to ask for their reaction to the program I'm going to outline in a few minutes.

I wonder—and I said this to the publishers that I spoke to on the phone—how many of our Ecco books would have been published in New York, even one obvious poetry title on our list, which has sold nearly twenty-five hundred copies in cloth. Now we've already broken even on that book, so that when the paperback edition comes out, which it will do in the spring, a year after the hardcover publication, that's all profit. That book was rejected three times, but maybe it would have found a home eventually.

The point is, there are only a few commercial publishers who will publish poetry. When we at *Antaeus* magazine receive over three thousand poems a month, and the prizes that end in book publication—the Yale Series, the Pittsburgh prize, and the Walt Whitman Award—are receiving up to two thousand manuscripts each year, it's obvious that there must be a few more publishing outlets set up. I don't see any reason to realistically think the commercial presses are going to do more than what they're doing already. Viking, Doubleday, Knopf, Harper & Row, Random House, Houghton Mifflin, and a few others ought to be applauded for what they do publish. As for the others—Simon & Schuster, Putnam, Grosset & Dunlap—the muse will take care of them.

The question is, Given the current situation, what can we do? I mean, this whole idea of being pragmatic at these conferences is a lot of talk, and then we all go back and that's the end of it. But it seems clear that talk and protest are fine, but they don't publish books of poetry.

I have a brief, but I hope complete, outline for a series of poetry books. I've gone over it numerous times and can find no reason for it not being implemented by next fall if we really want to do something. Before I get to this proposal, I want to say one more quick word about poetry sales. One big reason poetry doesn't sell well is because the poets who teach don't use books of contemporary poetry on their required reading lists. They use textbooks instead. If the thousands—and that is a low estimate—of poets teaching in American schools were to adopt volumes of poetry, sales would, to coin a phrase, skyrocket. Instead of textbooks raking in the money, books of poetry might become a financially viable publishing genre. It is very depressing to visit college bookstores and find no books of contemporary poetry on the shelves. I'm talking about the Midwest, I'm talking about California, Oregon, the East Coast. It is more depressing when my own students start complaining about how hard it is to find a publisher, and then I ask them how many books they bought in the last few months.

Someone pointed out this morning that there are more writers than readers. My question is, Why aren't these writers readers? And if *they* don't read or won't, who should or will?

So, let me just outline very quickly this idea that I have in my mind. I might have overlooked a whole aspect of publishing, which is possible. Anyway, the idea is called the National Poetry Series. I have it all outlined here, but I'll just read it quickly. It sounds more complicated than it is. Basically it's very simple, and the end product is that five books of poetry will be published each year in a quality paperback format. Each book will be printed by one of five participating university presses. When I was in the back room I was doing a little bit of research, and I don't know if I can lie here or not. Two or three more or less showed interest, and I would be willing to bet money that not only would you get five presses to do it but you would have people competing to be part of this series if it were set up in the right way.

Funding. That always seems to be a good topic of conversation at these conferences. The five books will be co-funded by the National Endowment for the Arts and the university presses. These fees are based on what I know from Ecco Press. The individual books should not cost more than $4,500 apiece, which require of each press $2,250, and a total grant for all five books from the NEA of $11,250, less than two individual grants they give out for poetry.

The selection. An original committee will be set up to select four judges. It will be the committee's aim to represent fairly —this is the difficult line in the proposal—the full spectrum of American poetry. Well. These judges will solicit one or more manuscripts and select one of the collections for publication. The poetry consultant to the Library of Congress will be the fifth judge. He will be responsible for selecting one book from a competition open to anyone who wishes to submit a manuscript. Now if the poetry consultant happens to be somebody like Stanley Kunitz, who's already judging the Yale, he can pass on his judgeship to somebody else, unless he wants to take on that too. He certainly has the energy. These competition manuscripts will be sent to one of the presses and then forwarded on to this poetry consultant. Ideally, the judges will write an introduction to the book they select, and the following will appear on each book, very simply on the cover: the National Poetry Series, selected by the judge—whoever it happens to be . This way the judge has to commit himself to a book and his name will be firmly implanted there. Each judge will serve for a term of two years and then give his judgeship to a person of his choice. The exception is the poetry consultant, who automatically becomes a judge for his term at the Library of Congress. The eligibility is completely open. There will be no age restriction, and both published and unpublished poets will be eligible. That means that if you've published five books and suddenly you find yourself without a publisher, this series does not exclude you. It's also open to first books.

The distribution. This is tricky, but luckily we have some commercial publishers here, and we can find out whether or not they're willing to participate in this. Each year a different commercial publisher will distribute, warehouse, and bill for the series, and receive as compensation 20 percent of the cover price. The authors will receive advances of $500 for their books, and paperback royalties of 7 percent. The press will receive 33 percent, and bookstores, the standard 40 percent. All five books ought to be published annually, as a group, from a single distributor. And that's the whole idea of it. It's a group of books of poems that comes out.

If this is to come to something lasting, we're going to have to respond to this proposal or accept the fact that talking is really a lot of fun and a good reason for a party. A simple metaphor is in this whole thing. Mark Twain said that he could never figure out why Moroccan women wore veils until they took them off. We've taken off some veils here and are going to continue to take off more veils. My only question, and that is a question which I'll leave you with, is: What are you going to do about it?

Zimmer:

Thank you, Dan. There's all this great energy and enthusiasm and a good plan, I think, an interesting plan. I think he's already selected the manuscripts, in fact.

Willard Lockwood, Wesleyan University Press, now.

Willard Lockwood:

Paul's gloomy introductory comments have raised in my mind several reactions, and I would like to begin with the most fundamental of them. All my remarks, as you might expect, are going to be from the point of view of the university press and will deal essentially with poetry as distinct from fiction.

My first reaction has to do with the role of university presses and how this role has changed over the last few decades. Although many aspects of university press publishing—many methods, techniques, procedures—are indistinguishable from those of commercial publishers, university presses are not commercial publishers. And what distinguishes them? Well, essentially, it's the why and the what that is published and not particularly the how. Traditionally, and this is very simplified, university presses began as outlets for the research and scholarship of their own campuses. In time their range expanded, and they became publishers of academic works from campuses generally, publishers primarily of monographic works and occasional works of regional interest and importance. Their visibility in the publishing world was slight and their profile was very low, and, whatever else they were, they were neither the actual nor the expected publishers of poetry, of fiction, or of creative works generally. I noticed, in this connection, that in Chester Kerr's report on university presses published in 1949, there's this comment: "The fields of fiction, verse, and drama have apparently been renounced or avoided by most presses as being outside their proper spheres of interest."

Well, as Paul has pointed out, times have indeed changed. Following World War II, in the fifties and perhaps even more in the sixties, there was a proliferation of university presses. There are roughly twice the number today as there were twenty-five years ago, and there has been a distinct and notable change in the character of university presses. These changes have been the result of both tug and push.

Universities have sought greater prestige and, recognizing the continuum of research and teaching and publication, have rounded out their academic enterprises by establishing presses. At the same time, commercial publishers, under an economic pressure which is mild by today's standards, began to find that their minimum viable print orders were rising. This left what I shall call a no-man's-land, a publishing level no longer profitable for the commercial publisher, but enticingly attractive to the university publisher. As the one-thousand to three-thousand initial print order became prohibitive to the trade house, it meant that academic publishers could address recently abandoned audiences which are refreshingly larger than those they had previously addressed.

As these conditions became history, the logical vehicles for short-run, serious books—that is, books that are not just monographic but serious nonacademic fare, including poetry—began to shift from Madison Avenue to Chapel Hill, to Norman, Oklahoma, to Berkeley, and to other university centers. University presses, in short, entered the no-man's-land and grasped the publishing opportunities deserted by the trade publishers, which were already beginning to be characterized by hyphenated imprints and amalgamated identities.

Not only was the legitimate area of university-press publishing expanding, the nature of the presses themselves was changing. Staffs, previously drawn almost exclusively from the academic community, were now being recruited from the ranks of professional, that is to say, commercial publishing. This brought greater publishing sophistication to the campuses, and it also brought, it seems to me, an important attitudinal change. This phenomenon on the university press staff level helped erode the notion, deserved or not, that university press books must be sufficiently serious as to be heavy and ponderous, if not outright dull. Only on this last Friday I was in conference with a professional writer, who, without realizing how patronizing he was being, described the books he wrote as books to be read, as distinct from those to be put on the shelf, by which he meant, of course, the books that we and other university presses traditionally publish.

But back to the point. The net result of this metamorphosis of role, particularly with respect to poetry, has, in my opinion, been salutary. Because of its innate prestige—and we have learned something more of this this morning as well—commercial publishers have not altogether abandoned poetry, but university presses have joined and enlarged the field. The outlets for publication of poetry have simply become more numerous. In addition, the recent increase in the number of small presses and of occasional imprints has further augmented, in a very significant way, the opportunities for poets to be published.

Now, I may be a Pollyanna, but I really do question the extent to which the present situation is really bad. Well, in a sense, of course, it is bad. As Paul has pointed out, the burden is being carried by publishers who operate either on a shoestring or at a deficit without the sort of diversification of list that generates profits with which to take up the slack which is inevitable in the publication of poetry. There is considerable consolation, however, in that this is occurring in a period of rising consciousness with respect to the arts in our society. I feel as if I am denying everything that I heard this morning, but I wrote this before I heard that. Moral support and, indeed, economic support are coming from sources hitherto nonexistent. Today's Wesleyan undergraduate, just to cite one example, can attend more poetry readings in a year than I, as an undergraduate at Wesleyan a generation ago, was able to hear in my whole academic career. Having said this, however, I must confess that it seems also to be true that as a society we are creating a gigantic spate of poets, and that no quantity of resources, no number of publishers, no amount of subsidy seems adequate to accommodate all of the poetry that is being produced.

So how do we survive in this period, those of us who are sticking to the job of publishing poetry? Aside from the obvious things like raising prices and juggling figures to make popular books subsidize significant books, our ultimate challenge, it seems to me, is to be tougher and tougher in selection, and then to be totally enthusiastic about what we publish, and then persist against all odds. We cannot be blind to economics, but we cannot be paralyzed by them either.

A brief institutional note: at Wesleyan, we have recently instituted a totally unorthodox and iconoclastic policy, and I'm delighted to be able to describe it at this forum. We now require, believe it or not, a three-dollar administrative and handling fee to accompany manuscripts which are to be considered for the Wesleyan poetry program. The only exception to this is that we waive the fee, very generously, for those poets whom we have already published. To date, we have had but three withdrawals from poets who feel affronted by this policy. Now either we are innovators or we are crazy, and only time will tell whether one or the other or both of these is true. The policy is solely to increase revenue, even though it cannot possibly turn deficit publishing into a break-even situation.

Now, since we've dwelt so heavily on statistics, I'm going to turn to some—most of which I've made up. According to some very fast and loose calculations drawn from the listing by the Academy of American Poets for books of poetry published in the spring season of this year, university presses and small presses account for some 86 percent of the poetry being published in this country, and that is either alarming or marvelous, depending on where you stand. By the same index, while we were combining poetry and drama figures this morning, it appears that, give or take, more than five hundred new and original books of poetry are being published this year. Well now, I think that's quite a bit of poetry. And it's hard to think, in the face of this, that times are uncommonly bad. I suspect that times are bad for poetry mostly in comparison with the lush late sixties. Now, just as Paul has put this in another perspective, I am confident the other panelists will as well, and I also look forward to their comments. Thank you.

Zimmer:

Will, I was just sitting here thinking, three dollars times sixteen hundred manuscripts is very interesting. Jeri Sherwood from Princeton University Press, now.

Jeri Sherwood:

Well, I have to say that every time I have listened to any one of you so far today, I have had to change my mind about what I was going to say, because you've pulled the rug out from under my feet—every single one of you. So I think that I will tell you a little bit about what Princeton does, mechanically, really.

As far as poetry goes, we really are an imaginary business. Our first two books of poetry will come out in December. We've had a second period of consideration, during which we got about three hundred manuscripts, and we rejected every one of them. I don't know whether that was crazy or sensible or what. It's silly to have a series if you haven't got anything to put in it, but it's equally silly to publish books that you don't happen to believe in.

The way we do it is to divide the year into two publishing seasons. We are getting, as I say, about three hundred manuscripts for each of these. I think we ought to adopt your three-dollar policy. I think it's a wonderful idea. We plan to publish one thousand copies in cloth and two thousand in paper, which we expect to last for three years. We base our publication plan on a three-year term. Of course, we'll be delighted if they don't last that long, and we will of course reprint them.

We're doing two poetry programs, actually: one in original poetry and one in poetry in translation. So out of a total list of about a hundred books a year, we hope to do up to four books of poetry, which isn't very much, but it's better than a kick in the face with a frozen boot, as they say.

My big worry is not so much the selection of the manuscript, but the completely different approach to marketing, distribution, advertising, and promotion generally that we have to learn about.. University presses do an awful lot of their advertising not in the ordinary places like the *New York Times*, and so on, but by direct mail. And that's no way to sell poetry. Most of our books are not easy to find on bookstore shelves. And that again is no way to sell poetry. We have to get the books on the shelf somehow, and I don't think we know how, and I think that the first few books are probably going to suffer. We hope to learn, in part, from what I hear from the rest of the speakers at this meeting.

I wonder, in contradistinction to the remarks of one gentleman this morning, why poetry books have to be beautiful. If we can produce more books more cheaply and get them out to the people who want them, why isn't that just as good? Why do they have to be physically objects of beauty? This is all part of what we're wondering about other books that we publish, scholarly books. We're doing some in typewriter offset, and so on. The authors don't like it, but surely they'd rather be published in a more casual form than not at all. What do you think about that, by the way?

Lockwood:

An interesting point.

Sherwood:

Thank you, thank you.

Lockwood:

How helpful that is.

Sherwood:

The business of simultaneous cloth and paper editions is a brand new step for us, because for our other sorts of books we have delayed paperback publication until we have sold a good many of the cloth copies. So the paperback doesn't eat into the cloth sales, and, from our point of view, with the size of the print runs that we have, it is perfectly true that you lose money on every paperback copy you sell.

That's awfully nuts and bolts stuff, but the few ideas I had were all preempted, so I think I'll stop there.

Zimmer:

Thank you very much, Jeri. I think there is a real question about the publication of beautiful books of poetry and a real question about whether we can continue to do it or not, but maybe we can face this a little bit later.

Dudley Randall with the Broadside Press in Detroit.

Dudley Randall:

My remarks will be rather disjointed. I have made comments on the talk of Mr. Zimmer, and I have some comments on some of the panel's points, which have been raised by speakers on this panel and on the morning panel, and I will take these points in order.

First of all, that question about buyers of books. I read recently about a poetry contest where there were over one thousand entries sent in, indicating that over one thousand people were interested in poetry. But when the winner was selected and the winning book was published, only about two or three hundred books were sold. So these people like to write poetry, but they don't buy it. And I think if we like to write poetry we should buy it.

About the beauty of books of poetry. I believe the books should be legibly printed. I believe the type should be legible. But I don't think that the type should be intrusive so that it makes the reader forget about the poem he's reading. As one famous typographer said, "The best type is that invisible type which doesn't call attention to itself and detract attention from the content of the type." I would prefer a book without an illustration on the cover. An artist will tell you that one picture is worth a thousand words, but I would answer that one word can inspire in the reader a thousand pictures. Instead of one picture that the painter presents to everybody, one word will present a thousand pictures to a thousand readers. So I'm not so much for pictures or illustrations in books as I'm for just good, legible, and graceful type on the cover.

About paperback books being reviewed. In Helen Vendler's recent column of reviews, she reviewed a Broadside Press book not too unfavorably, and it was a paperback book. In fact, all of our books come out first in paperback. Only our most popular authors are printed simultaneously in hardcover and paperback. And that's because of necessity. We don't have much money, so we have to do the best with what we have.

We're not worried about commercial publishers. We don't criticize commercial publishers because we know what they are. They are commercial. Poets have always had a hard time, and especially black poets. Gwendolyn Brooks said in one of the courses that she taught, "In the anthology of American poetry, there was not one black poet. There was one Jewish poet." When I was teaching at the University of Michigan, the English Department asked me to put together a small anthology of black poetry, because in the anthologies they used in their courses in modern poetry, American poetry, and contemporary poetry, the students had complained because there were no black poets, or very few black poets in them. So, therefore, I put together a little anthology called *Black Poetry; a Supplement to Anthologies Which Exclude Black Poets.* The title of that is self-explanatory. That explains why we need black studies departments in our colleges, why we need black literature courses, and why we need black history courses. I could go on about our historians, but I won't.

In Mr. Zimmer's talk, he mentioned writers like James Dickey or Richard Brautigan, who are swept up by the big presses after they have proven themselves hot. I would question James Dickey and Richard Brautigan, why they let themselves be swept up by the big presses when it's the little presses that published them first. A contrary example is Gwendolyn Brooks, who was published by Harper & Row. She gave her books to Broadside Press not because she was dissatisfied with Harper & Row—it had always treated her fairly and well—but because she wanted to help a small black press. This is the way that some established and good-selling authors can help the small presses—by giving their books to the small presses. She gave us one book, *Riot,* for which she accepts no royalties. All the permissions, all the income that we get from the book go to Broadside Press. She gets none of it herself. And that is one way that established writers can help small presses.

About the number of books sold. There are some of our poets whose printings are regularly 5,000 copies. We don't have to worry about whether the books will sell because we know that we can put out a printing of 5,000 copies and they will sell. If we had more money, we would put out a printing of 10,000 copies, and we would be confident that their books would sell. For instance, I wrote a history of Broadside Press in 1969, and I figured up the amount of Don Lee's books that had sold, and they came to 75,-000. This is now 1975, so I believe the number of his books that we have sold is around 150,000 or 200,000. He sells and others of our poets sell because he and they have something meaningful to say to the people.

Mr. Zimmer spoke about grants being made to university and small presses. At first, Broadside Press would not ask for grants because we thought we would go it alone. But around the fifteenth of every month, when I get the taxes—we get taxes, local taxes, state taxes, federal taxes—if I have a thousand dollars in my checking account, by the time I have paid these taxes and made the payroll, we don't have any money left to do anything else. So we have applied for grants, and we got a grant from the National Endowment for the Arts, which enabled us to publish three chapbooks. And that's another way that small presses can be helped. I think that we don't have to publish big, fat, thick books. All of these chapbooks were only 16 pages long. If a poet writes for a lifetime and he produces five poems that live, he has done a great thing. So I don't think we have to strive for big thick books of 64 pages or 80 pages or 200 pages. I think we can put out books of 16 and 24 pages, and they won't intimidate people, especially the audience for which our poets write, many of whom are nonreaders. People will buy what is meaningful to them. The other day I spent $3.15 for a pint of whiskey because I wanted to drink. People spend that much money every week or every day for whiskey because they want it. Once I received an ad for a book that cost $49.00. The first thing I did was to reach for my checkbook and send an order for the book. The reason why was because the title of the book was *How to Make Money Publishing Books.* If you want a book or anything enough, you will pay for it, no matter what the price is. If you don't have the money, you will say, "I would have bought it if I had the money." But if you really want the book, you will buy it. That's why I think it's up to the poet. A lot of what needs to be done is up to the poets. They need to make their work meaningful to people. The reason Don Lee sells 100,000 or 150,000 or 200,000 books is because he has made his poetry meaningful to his audiences. He talks about survival in America, and that relates to the people who read or who hear him read. I think poets should stop being obscure, and here I know I'm treading on dangerous ground. I don't mean that a poet should not be deep, should not be meaningful, should not be serious. But, for instance, if a poet has the subject of a sentence in line one and you don't reach the verb until line six, by the time you get to line six you have forgotten what the poet was talking about. I think we should make our work clear so the people can understand. Don Lee and I were talking several years ago about clarity. We said: "If you have something important to tell the people, how should you write?" And we agreed that if you have something important that you want people to get, you should tell it in a clear fashion. Otherwise, what's the use of writing if people can't understand what you write?

I think that the poets should also help to sell the books. The best time and place to sell a book is when the poet has just given a reading. For some reason, it brings the poetry more to life, and people are eager to buy the book. Lee used to carry boxes of books around on airplanes to his various readings, and he would get a sister in the audience to sell the books for him. So, as has been suggested, he would not demean himself by selling the books himself. And that's a very good way to sell your books—at your readings.

I guess that's all I have to say. Those are all my notes. If I have any more to say, I'll say it later.

Zimmer:

Thank you very much, Mr. Randall. I'm going to continue to buy poetry books, but I think I'll continue to buy whiskey also. Jack Shoemaker of the Sand Dollar Press.

Jack Shoemaker:

It becomes apparent that the way to make money in publishing is to publish a book called *How to Make Money in Publishing* and sell it for $49. I hadn't thought of that.

I've got responses to several different points, and then one suggestion. I too would applaud the commercial presses for what they do and think of this as a time when access to print is extraordinary. But the flaws in commercial publishing are obvious. It was mentioned this morning that the notion of quantitative growth in this country without qualitative knowing is wasting the planet and wasting the country. Conglomerates, the fast-buck publishing, the big-book mentality, and the piggyback-book mentality have ground New York down to where it's worried about itself. Now there were many of us in the small-press world that were worried about New York long before it got the message. We have attempted, as small-press publishers, to revive a cottage industry. I publish my books out of my household budget. I believe that virtually all other small-press publishers do the same. I have a great faith in the people of this country and in the people in the small-press world. We are now noticing that not only are early books of poetry difficult to place in New York City but first novels and books with a potential audience of around three thousand copies are also exceedingly difficult to place. I think what will happen will be a birth of the medium-size publisher—I used to think of New Directions as a medium-size press. Alan Swallow worked all his life creating a medium-size press. One can make money with print runs of about three thousand copies. I was told by Mike Bessie at Atheneum that poetry existed at Atheneum because of the sole effort of one man, that he, as a hobby, literally, took these books home with him nights, copy edited them, proofread them, worked out the contracts, and handled the book all the way up through the printing stage. And yet that is a house—Atheneum—that is extraordinarily successful from my standpoint. They have Merwin, who must be a best-seller. If you break down the conglomerate notions and try to pay three salaries, four salaries, a very small overhead, then it is viable to publish three thousand copies. It's viable for me to publish one thousand copies, or five hundred. I can make a small profit. There is a small press called Black Sparrow which has been the model for several efforts in New York. Their average print run now is probably ranging up to about two thousand copies. They publish a simultaneous cloth and paperback. They publish a signed cloth edition and price it $15 and utilize the profits from that, which they sell to libraries and collectors, to underwrite the paperback edition. John Martin, that publisher, supports himself at a reasonable level and has to work very hard. He is a single man with a part-time employee, but it works. And he has published over 120 books of poetry since 1970. That's what I see coming, that's what I intend to do. That's what I know the small-press field—a certain part of it—is moving toward, and I would not despair.

A couple of other comments on the university presses' method of sale of poetry. It's been my experience, and I think the experience of the small press, that direct mail is your best method of sale; that, more and more, it seems, we have been unable to utilize bookstores, and we have gone almost totally now to direct mail and word of mouth, as Daniel mentioned.

I'd be glad to answer direct questions about the small-press field, but I think I've taken enough time and I'll just wait for responses.

Zimmer:

Mark Vinz of Dacotah Territory Press.

Mark Vinz:

There's a real advantage to coming last because I can say all my ideas have been used. But there are a few things I'd like to add, especially to what Jack said.

My press is very small. It grew out of my magazine, which I've been doing for five years. We started a chapbook series two years ago to publish some writers in our area at the beginning—upper Midwest—some very talented young writers who needed a kind of calling card. Although this series was expanded—now I'm doing some full-length books and anthologies—I'm really very much of a newcomer to the idea of a small press. But I think that much of what I have to say applies equally to small presses and magazines.

I've heard a lot about the idea of audience. I think most magazines in this country have some sort of regional basis. I don't mean they're regional in the worst sense of the word, but they have a kind of regional tie, a regional identity, regional source of money. And I think those of us doing magazines and small presses perhaps are aware of an audience that is invisible to New York, that is invisible to some of the large distributors, perhaps even to some of the university presses. That gives me a kind of hope, too, just in the manner in which I'm able to distribute and sell out everything that I print to an audience, which, to many other people, is an invisible one.

Second, I am hopeful because of a kind of reeducation, I think, that's going on all over the country, through things like the Poets-in-the-Schools program and like the number of poets going out and giving readings. We are gradually becoming reeducated to what a poem is. The child in the classroom doesn't have to feel ashamed to like poetry. He can read a poem by a living author. That's getting more and more possible. And I think that goes back to that invisible audience I'm talking about.

Another thing, a link to a larger publishing house that you mentioned, Alan Swallow. There are ways. What I don't want to see is large presses of any kind close themselves off to possibilities because of some sense of business or profit. The distinction that's made usually—by a lot of people, anyway, such as Richard Kostelanetz—between large- and small-press publishing is the idea of being commercial or not being commercial. Well, to give you a practical example from my experience: Alan Swallow did, three years ago, the collected shorter poems of the poet Thomas McGrath. And Swallow never got around to releasing the paperback for one reason or another, and the hardback was $8.50. Tom was very upset because nobody was buying it, and most of the people that he wanted to buy the book and read the book didn't have $8.50. So, by arrangement with Swallow, which worked out very easily, I printed a paperback sampler, fifty pages, fifty poems. Tom picked fifty, I picked fifty, and we haggled. And so I think that's a way where small press and large press can work together. We're into our third printing of this now, and that leads me to my third point in terms of audience, and that's cost.

I agree with a lot of what I've heard about people. The people who submit manuscripts don't buy poetry books. I'm guilty of that myself, although I'm in a good position of being a magazine editor and getting magazines and books from all over the country—more than I can possibly read—which I in turn give to my students. But I think that's something that small presses can do: make available to an audience good work, top work, nicely done, nicely designed, at much less cost than some of the large presses. Again, maybe that's partly because of a more regional orientation.

The second thing I want to say about audience has become a very personal kind of gripe with me. I was a panelist in Cleveland this summer at the Associated Councils of the Arts, and one of the things we talked about there was simply coverage of the arts. I think that's one of the things all small-press people have been struggling with for a long, long time: getting a book review not in the *New York Times Book Review* but in their local papers. I found that one review in the *Fargo Forum,* which sounds like a Johnny Carson show, sold, within a week, two hundred copies of a chapbook. And yet sometimes the people who totally ignore small presses are the people in whose area the small press is happening. And I think, again, maybe we still are a little bit too oriented to either coast. I'm a midwesterner, and maybe I'm defensive about that, but the marvelous thing about small presses and magazines, it seems to me, is that things are happening all over the country, and sometimes we fail to take that into consideration. So I've put all of that in just to kind of temper what I said about the idea of the invisible audience. I think there's more of an audience there, at least I know more of that audience.

The last thing that I want to say, in a more practical sense, again, comes down to a kind of something that can happen in a region and not nationally—or at least not right now. A group of us, where I am in Minnesota, got together and formed something called the Plains Distribution Service, which is two parts. One part is eight midwestern magazine editors: one from each of the Dakotas, one from Iowa, two from Wisconsin, and three from Minnesota, who are working together. We're doing common advertising, brochures, posters. We've got a mailing coming up of 8,000—common subscription, all kinds of things. Distribution has been a major problem with all publishing in this country. I think some of the small-press people have some of the best ideas about distribution and really need to be listened to.

The second half of our project—the brochure is hot off the press—we're doing a booklist, again, because our funding base is midwestern. This is limited to the Midwest as far as selecting books goes. Now, the booklist will go all over the country. There are fifteen books by midwestern authors, including Roland Flint, who's now living in Washington, D.C., and publishes with a D.C. press—a very fine press, Dryad. There's a university press book, Lucien Stryk's *Heartland II; Poets of the Midwest;* Daniel Lusk's handbook for Poets-in-the-Schools; *Margins* magazine, a very fine small-press review from Milwaukee. It's a very mixed list. This booklist—brochure—is going out all over the country. It will be done on the order of a book club. It's not really a book club. The list will be changed quarterly with a cumulative catalog coming out of it. So, in a practical sense, this idea of audience again. Some of the things that I've been involved with, and from the small-press people I know and the small-press meetings I've gone to, I think there tends to be a lot more optimism and a lot more doing than from some of the other camps.

Zimmer:

I won't attempt to summarize what has just been said. A lot has been said. And I must say that we are people who are fortunate enough to operate as small publishers and university press publishers, who don't have to deal with the philosophy of the big hit. We don't have to contend with it. There are, at long last, excellent people with the commercial publishers, and I'm sorry that so many brickbats have been dealt today, because I say kudos to those good people who are keeping the faith with the commercial publishers, too.

I'd like to say something to what Mr. Laughlin said about the number of poets in this country and the impossibility of dealing with all of them. I believe there is a good deal of truth to this. It seems to me that we have passed out of an age of masters; they have all passed in the last ten years. There are apparently, at least at this point, not many masters that are going to replace them. And nevertheless I believe it is true also that we are in an age when there are great numbers of fine writers. It's an age of, one might say, competence, and I think it's an exciting time to be at work. It's likened to maybe the seventeenth century. I can think of no other time for it, when there were so many good writers around. What we must concern ourselves with is how we can serve these people and, above all, how we can make certain that the best of all of this is published—that very important business of selectivity.

Finally, Dan made an interesting proposal, and I think perhaps some people would like to address themselves to it from the audience. I would like to make an even more outrageous suggestion, in some ways. I won't go into great detail, but it will certainly be chewed up for a while, at any rate: the possibility that commercial publishers are not able—many of them admit they're not able—to pioneer new talent. What about some plan being worked out wherein commercial publishers can give money to small presses and university presses so that they can do the pioneering for them?

Okay. I'm going to call for questions from the audience. I would be very appreciative if you would stand up, say your name, and address your question to one particular panel member. Please. . . . We've stunned you all. Yes.

Audience:

Is it a custom among publishing houses to trade lists with other publishers, mailing lists for potential buyers or at least very precious items that one publisher hides from the others?

Vinz:

The people I've been working with are very good about sharing lists and putting lists together from other sources. John Milton from the *South Dakota Review* had a marvelous idea. He got a list of all the dentists in South Dakota and sold a lot of subscriptions to *South Dakota Review* for dentists' waiting rooms.

Zimmer:

Yes.

Henry Taylor:

I want to ask Mrs. Sherwood a question about something I saw about the Princeton series in a newsletter, to the effect that most of the poems in manuscript have to be unpublished. Does that mean . . . is that a mistake of some kind?

Sherwood:

No, it isn't a mistake. We started out by saying that any poet submitting a manuscript should have published some of his poems someplace, and the more we thought about it, the more meaningless that became. I mean, it could have been their high school yearbook, you know, or anything. Now we hope that at least half of the poems in a manuscript will have been unpublished. We're putting the emphasis the other way around, in other words.

Taylor:

But I don't know why.

Sherwood:

You don't know why. Well, at the stage we are at, I think that we should concentrate on publishing material that is not available in any other place when we do a book. In other words, we want at least half of it to be completely fresh and not have been seen elsewhere. That doesn't seem unreasonable to me.

Taylor:

Thank you.

Zimmer:

Yes. Peter.

Davison:

I'd like to ask a question that's been on my mind for a long time. I think that you people this afternoon were absolutely right, you know much more about selling poetry than commercial publishers do. I think if you took any book we published, you could probably sell 50 percent or 100 percent more copies than we could, but there's one thing that has occurred to me as a possible way of dividing up the territory. I'd like to get your reactions. I'm directing this first at Ecco Press and Wesleyan. Isn't it conceivable that the short book—the chapbook, the slim volume—is possibly the right medium for a small publisher or university press, and the large collected volume—the 128-page, 256-page volume—is the proper unit for the trade publisher?

Halpern:

Let me say something about that. That means, up here, that we have to depend on you to publish the larger collection. We can do the small ones all right, but are you going to do the big ones? I hear you've turned down some. The point is that this idea of chapbooks, like David Godine's very fine little talk here, pointed out some very important things. But now, you make this differentiation between a chapbook and a full collection. I'm not talking about selected or complete—just regular books of poetry. Louise Glück's book is forty-five pages. Now that sells for us like a regular book of poetry—it sells for $6.95. But that could also have been a chapbook; with a few less pages, it could have been maybe thirty-eight pages. So, now, would you consider that a full collection of poetry?

Davison:

I consider that a slim volume. I'm talking about the distinction between slim volumes and selected or collected.

Halpern:

Oh, selected or collected. I would have the same question in the end. Would you do the books after they were done by the small publishers?

Davison:

Yes.

Halpern:

Given the current situation? How can you say yes, you don't know what books they are.

Davison:

I'm sorry, we're misunderstanding each other.

Halpern:

No doubt.

Davison:

We have published books—my firm has published books—of selected poems that have been previously published by other publishers. Yes, we are considering books that are—have in part been—published in chapbook form. I am simply thinking, for example, of the publishing history of William Carlos Williams that Mr. Laughlin was referring to this morning. It's not a good case, but it's relevant to this. First, think of lots of small books published all over; then imagine bringing them together in a coherent series of books under the New Directions imprint; and then, at last, sadly or happily, the large collected poems under the Random House imprint. Is that sensible enough? Perhaps you can speak to that, too.

Halpern:

I want to say one thing about that. One thing is that the small presses, then, will spend the money to create the reputation of these people so that you can skim off the.... No, I am not being facetious about this, Peter.

Davison:

As long as the copyright law is passed, we would be sharing it.

Halpern:

All right, let's take a case in point, like James Tate. Okay, now. You published two of his volumes.

Davison:

Right.

Halpern:

You decided not to publish the third, for whatever reason. But you would be willing to do a selected edition of his work, right? So he's the perfect poet in terms of what you're talking about.

Davison:

In principle, yes.

Halpern:

Okay. But now, see, he's against it, as a poet, because he decides that if you don't want to do his new book, why should you get to do a selected? So he's making that decision.

Davison:

Sure.

Lockwood:

Well, with all respect to Peter, I don't think this is dividing the territory. I think that if we publish a poet and we "stay with him"—we keep publishing him—it seems proper to go on with a collected or a selected or both, and it's our idea and we want to do it. I don't know why we should go to our big brother. By the same token, we all have the same access to the mails and all of this, and, in fact, we could discuss betwixt us poetic loyalties, changing from one house to another. These things happen. I don't think this is something that is up for the commercial publisher and the small press or university press to decide. As has just been pointed out, the poet has a great deal to do with it. I don't think it is dividing the territory. I think that the appropriate book in its time can be handled by anybody who is terribly enthusiastic about that poet and about that poetry.

Zimmer:

I would just like to add to that that we're getting to the point with the Pitt series where we're going to be doing some selected and collected poems, and I would be blind with rage if one of them decided to take their selected or collected somewhere else, after all of this. I must admit that it would be very difficult. A lot of heart goes into all of that business, and—yes?

David Godine:

I think the sword often cuts both ways. Our house is purely

pragmatic, and when we publish poetry, we publish it like everything else. We said if we're not going to lose money on it, then
how are we going to do it? And when we did the chapbooks,
there were three answers that we came up with. The first thing
was that we tended to do very well-known poets along with unknown poets, because we knew how the system worked. And we
knew if any of our salesman went to a store and said, "Look, this
series, we know it is true, is unknown, but also there is X. J.
Kennedy, John Hollander, Thom Gunn, Marvin Bell," and no
matter how stupid the book buyer was, he'd pay attention to the
series. And we are going to get unknown poets along with
known poets. That's number one. Two, we knew that we had to
keep the price at four dollars. That was the top of the market if
we wanted them in hardcover, which they are, which means they
have to be produced, as any of you know in the trade, for eighty
cents—not a penny more. But by doing them in editions of 2,500
each, we were essentially doing a print run of five times 2,500—
12,500. And the economies of doing 12,500 are substantial as
opposed to the economies of doing 2,500 books—all printed at
once, all bound at once, et cetera. And the third thing was that we
knew we couldn't get Hollander, let's say, away from Atheneum,
or Marvin Bell or Scott Momaday away from Harper's, but we
knew too that frequently the better trade houses got manuscripts
that they really wanted to publish, but they couldn't do it. They
couldn't fit them on the list. They said, "Come back in 1984, and
we'll print your poems." But they knew we were a source, and I
think that other people publishing chapbooks have found the
same. Knopf, Atheneum, Harper's don't mind at all if poetry's
been published before and frequently will go out in terrific sub-
mission from these houses. So I think that idea, if you're smart,
you know, can work with mutual benefits in both directions.

Audience:

May I ask Mr. Randall, how well have your tapes of poetry
sold?

Randall:

They haven't sold very well, but they've sold better than we antic-
ipated. When I first put them out they were in groups of fifty.
They were autographed by the poets, and that was all. But then
we found out that after we had sold fifty, we still got orders. So
we put out extra copies, but they don't sell in big quantities. They
are more of a supplement to the books than separate editions in
large quantities. Does that answer your question?

Zimmer:

Yes.

Eshleman:

I'd like to address the thing that Peter brought up a little bit ago. One complication on that is that I think some of the most adventuresome poets since the Second World War—and I have in mind poets like Louis Zukofsky, Charles Olson, Theodore Enslin, Robert Kelly—have written extremely long and open-ended series that would be quite a complication, given the sort of thing you're mentioning. Just last week, Black Sparrow Press, for example, published a 415-page poem of Robert Kelly's. Recently, the Elizabeth Press brought out in four volumes—that comes to around 1,000 pages—a long work by Enslin called *Forms.* So I don't think that if you received a 300- or 400-page manuscript by a person in his forties, you would possibly be in a position to be able to back it, and that's why it's going into the other presses.

In conjunction with that, I'd like to mention that one of the ways that Black Sparrow was able to do the Kelly manuscript was that it was set by Kelly himself on a compositor. The compositor printing really looks terrific, I think. Unless you're really finicky, you can't tell it from hot type. So I think that one of the things that's going to come in more and more is the avoiding of that middle-man printer. Poets, by getting together and using compositors, could actually set their own work, and this would also give them a certain kind of control over the work. There's a very interesting essay by Robert Duncan in *Maps,* in which he talks about the idea of the book—losing control when he should have control over the way that his work appears. And this is something that can reduce costs considerably.

Zimmer:

Yes. Mr. Kunitz?

Kunitz:

I have a communication that I want to read, so I think I'll step up to the mike.

Zimmer:

Are we finished here or do we continue?

Kunitz:

I think we can continue for a few minutes.

One of the persons we invited to the conference for this panel was Chester Kerr, director of the Yale University Press, and he was unfortunately unable to come. But we did want him to talk about the Yale Poetry Series—the Yale Series of Younger Poets—and he sent me, as current editor of this series, a memorandum about the series that I think will be of interest to this audience and to the panel. I'll quote from it a few paragraphs.

Before I do that, I'd like to say something about some of the things that have been said this afternoon. I'm interested that the panelists out of the small presses and the university presses seem, on the whole, more affirmative, more positive, more helpful, than the trade publishers. And I think there's a clue to it in the fact that they are perhaps doing the work of the future in relation to poetry. And maybe that is the direction that poetry will largely turn to. It would be my guess that that is the ultimate solution of the problem of poetry publishing. I think that the suggestion that there should be a symbiotic relationship between trade publishers and small presses is a good one. I'd like to see that explored. I would like to see the major presses interested in publishing adopt small presses in regions other than their own to achieve some of the decentralization that I think is highly important. And the fact that the major publishers are concentrated on the eastern seaboard is, I think, one of the prime reasons for the failure to reach the general population. So if we could achieve this kind of marriage, I think it would be all to the good, and I wish there could be some further exploration of that through various funding agencies.

Now about the Yale Series. It's the oldest poetry series in existence. It's been going on since 1920, so it is now fifty-five years old, and the seventy-first book that has just been selected and will be published next spring is by Carolyn Forché—some of you may know her work. Maura Stanton, who will read tonight, was the seventieth choice. I don't know whether she's in the audience or not, I think she is. Now—oh, one thing to say. Annually, we get between seven hundred and nine hundred volumes submitted, and I must say that I make an effort to go through them all. This I believe in with great conviction, because I don't believe that a judge in a contest of this sort should delegate the task of weeding out all of the manuscripts to others. The best, the most interesting, the most original manuscript may be lost in the shuffle, and what he gets will be a kind of conventional taste in the end—a meeting of minds, which, in this case, would probably mean the omission of the rare book that ought to be given special attention.

One of the reasons, I think, that the Yale Series has achieved a certain degree of prestige in the publishing world is the consistency of taste. The judges have been solo judges, they have not been a committee, and they have operated in the series over a period of years so that there is a tradition established, a chain of being, that I think is all to the good. There are other ways of doing it as other contests have shown. Now, to Chester Kerr's letter.

This series was started in 1920 at the instigation of none other than Clarence "Life with Father" Day, brother of the founder of the press, George Parmly Day. For the first several years, the project was edited by members of the Yale English Department. Then in 1925, William Alexander Piercy took over. Piercy was succeeded by Stephen Vincent Benét (1933-42), Archibald MacLeish (1942-45), W. H. Auden (1946-58), Dudley Fitts (1959-69), and Stanley Kunitz thereafter. [Not permanently thereafter, I assure you.]

Beginning with Starbuck, the first Fitts choice, we made what has turned out to be a bright decision: to publish simultaneously in paper and in cloth. Up to that time—1956—we used to sell an average of 750 to 1,000 in cloth. We still sell those; 1,157 copies in the last fifteen years, bumped upward by Alan Dugan, who won both the National Book Award and the Pulitzer Prize, and whose volume sold 3,000 in cloth, plus an [this is for the whole series, beginning with Fitts's choice in '56, paperback sales] average of 4,350, plus approximately 1,157 in cloth, as an average for the whole series during the last eighteen years. I think that's fairly good, with Tate and Casey running to 8,800 and 7,000, respectively [that is, James Tate and Michael Casey].

The press has subsidized the venture whenever necessary, and in recent years has more than broken even. We were—and are—immensely proud of this contribution to American poetry [and then a little puff], the oldest and good enough today to withstand all the recent competition.

Let me say that out of the submissions, of those seven hundred to nine hundred that we get annually, I find that there are usually a minimum of six manuscripts that I feel should be published— must be published. The unfortunate circumstance is that I have authority to select only one. I do try to reach out to other publishers and tell them about these books that should be published and have been pretty lucky in seeing them through to publication with other publishers. I think that sort of relationship should be encouraged, and publishers who find that they cannot publish a book of poetry that they truly admire should try to help that poet or that fiction writer get published elsewhere. If there were more of that sharing, I think that fewer really first-rate books would be lost in the shuffle. And that's something that happens. That's about it. Thank you very much.

Zimmer:

I'd like to comment on the last thing that Mr. Kunitz said. It is indeed extremely important that writers, creative people, be generous with each other in this way. I think it's essential. Do we have more questions? Yes.

Williams:

Well, I'm Galen Williams, and I'm an administrator, and I believe in lists, and I was trying to see how many we could get on a list this afternoon. We have twenty-five applications to the NEA in fellowships; there's twelve hundred that came in from the individual writing program at New York State; there's Pittsburgh, two thousand; there's Yale, seven hundred to nine hundred; there's the Whiteman Prize at one thousand to sixteen hundred applications. That's eight thousand names right there of writers, and—

Zimmer:

Yes, there is duplication.

Williams:

But we have the basis of a list, plus the Poets & Writers list, which at the moment is about twenty-five hundred poets and fiction writers, forty-five hundred purchasers of the directory, and about five hundred important people, clubs, editors, reviewers. It's about eight thousand; so right there we have about sixteen thousand names in this country, minus, say, maybe three thousand duplications. Maybe it would be worth it to start processing these on addressographs and get a master list.

Zimmer:

Many of them are rejected, disgruntled poets, however.

Williams:

Well, on that point, I wonder, when you apply—taking Mr. Lockwood's idea of asking for three dollars—why not ask for. . . . I was trying to think, if you could buy your favorite book of the year and send that, but then the NEA would have a terrible storage problem. What if you Xeroxed your favorite poems, then it would be ripping it off. If you tore off the title page that wouldn't do any good. I don't know how they would prove it. A sales slip—

Unidentified:

They would offer a proof of purchase.

Williams:

Yes, and then another way would be to have the NEA or the states purchase books that were chosen and then sent to the rejection people with a note. At least there would be an audience.

Zimmer:

Galen Williams was suggesting that there is a great mass of sales information that could be shared by publishers of poetry through the sharing of the lists of people who've entered contests and so forth. I think it's a very interesting idea. We've used our list, in the past, of people who've entered the U.S. Award Contest, and I fondly remember one business reply envelope stuffed with our mailing piece, and back into it somebody had scrawled on it with a black pencil, "Shove it." But the next one bought a copy, I'm sure. Yes, please.

Wayne Dodd:

I love that suggestion of Ms. Williams's, but I'm getting a little disturbed by the spinoff from Mr. Lockwood's suggestion about what Wesleyan is doing to generate money by getting three dollars. Everyone seems to be picking up on that, and it disturbs me. And so I'd like to ask a polemical question of the group, but I don't want an answer to it. I want everyone to think about it, if there isn't something very conceited about this attempt to feed on the need of serious writers to get published into a shrinking source of publication, and I'm disturbed by that. I mean I understand the need of Wesleyan to handle a mass of manuscripts, but . . .

Lockwood:

Wayne, may I respond. Let me tell you that I'll share a secret with you all, and that is that part of the rationalization of this was really that the bad poets really ought to support the good poets. And we realize that we turn down so many more than we take, you see, that by accepting three dollars from each, good poetry is driving out bad poetry, and bad poetry is paying for it. That's our justification.

Dodd:

I understand somewhat, but I don't like the way this sounds.

Zimmer:

I did react to that earlier, I must say, but I'm pleased to report that we have considered this possibility in the past at Pitt, and we have rejected it. Yes.

Stanley Bergen:

I'm the editor of the *Ohio Review.* I have a question for Mrs. Sherwood. Before I direct this to you, I'd like to make a more general observation. I think the most exciting thing that's happened today has been generated from the table on the right, where we have three people who actually believe that there is a market out there, and they're finding the market. And I think they stand in direct contrast to the trade publishers, the commercial people this morning, who are managing to effect a self-fulfilling prophecy that there isn't a market out there. It disturbs me. I'm finishing up a trade book on McGuffey readers. I've been asked by my publisher—I haven't finished the manuscript yet— I've been asked to start plugging the book already. How many poets in here have been asked to plug books of poetry? How many trade publishers have promoted books of poetry like that or tried it one time? Tried getting Galway Kinnell on commercial television, reading? I think that would help all poetry, to do something like this, to actually try this tack. And I think the small-press people here are giving some ideas. They're showing us that if you look for the market, you can find the market, you can make the market. Now for that other observation—question. We accept in our magazine something much smaller than one-half of one percent of the poems that are submitted. And I've seen poets who've put together manuscripts submitted for book publication where they have used only half of the poems that they have had published in small magazines, in *Salmagundi,* in *Iowa Review,* in *Field, Ohio Review,* and so on. Some of these may have won Borestone Awards or been included. Why? Why did you have a requirement that, let's say, half of the work should be new and untried on any kind of audience or must be absolutely virgin? I don't understand that. You said you thought it was perfectly sensible and reasonable. I find it inexplicable.

Sherwood:

Well, I feel rather limp about that. We had to start someplace, and we didn't want to be publishing books that were rehashes of stuff that people could find in journals or any other place. Now, this may be completely wrong; we may change our whole approach. I really don't know. Our first two books haven't even come out yet. We don't know what's going to happen; this is all very experimental. We asked a great many people for their advice, and we got about as many different kinds of advice as the number of people we asked. It was all totally conflicting with itself and each other, and finally, I said, "The hell with it. I'm going to do it my way and if it doesn't work, we'll change." This may well be a thing that we change. I don't know. As I say, this is where we began. It seemed reasonable to us at the time, and I'm going to wait and see what happens. I can't answer any better than that.

Zimmer:

I'm sorry, I was guilty there of not repeating that question. I'll do that from now on. Yes, please.

Judith Sherwin:

I would like to ask the people on the panel collectively—since you sound as if you feel that you're successful at selling poetry books, which is a wonderful sound to be hearing in this place—what effort is being made to coordinate the distribution of your books with the public appearances of your writers, or do you find that an irrelevant activity? How much of a percentage of your sales is done through a catalog or through a mail order? How much is done through live appearance?

Randall:

Poets & Writers sends us notices of places where the poets are going to read, with the name of a person to get in touch with. If our poets also do that, we will write the person and send him a catalog and try to get books down there to sell. As I said before, some of our poets carry their books with them, and it's not necessary to do that kind of coordination. What was the second part of your question?

Audience:

What percentage of your sales, about, would be through mail order or listing in a catalog or through live appearance?

Randall:

We don't go that much into statistics. We do have a catalog which we send out with a coupon on it, and we get the coupons back in the mail. We do like to sell things through mail order. We call it prepaid because that means it eliminates the paperwork and it's good for our cash flow. Those two are not the biggest proportion of our sales, though. We sell quite a few books to colleges because many of our poets are used in classes, and we sell quite a few to libraries. But we do look with favor on prepaid orders for the reasons that I've told you.

Zimmer:

The question was, What kind of an effort do we make to be certain that a poet is able to publicize his own book, to take it with him to readings and so forth? Is that right? That's the first part of the question. And the second part of the question was, What kind of percentage of our sales comes from direct mail and non-bookstore kind of activity? Right? Who else would like to answer that question? Anyone else?

Shoemaker:

I can give rough statistics. I think about 20 percent of my titles are sold by some public appearance. Either the poet is a teacher or has a public reading. I would make an observation that I've put on poetry readings for the last ten years in various parts of this country. It's much easier to get small presses to take a chance on you and send you the poet's work than it is to get major commercial houses to send the work. So predominantly you see a table filled with small-press books. Seventy percent of my business is by mail, and it's designed by mail. I would prefer to deal that way. I think one might make an observation that as a publisher in the old days, you were a bridge between the author and the audience. I must know a good fifth of my clientele on a first-name basis, and I try to keep responsive to that audience. I like the relationship, and I think maybe the commercial houses have maintained contact with the writers, but maybe they've lost contact with the potential audience.

I also wanted to make a note about your symbiotic relationships. It was always my opinion that that's what was going on. I was publishing the early books of a poet, and eventually he would have his big books published in New York. A couple of things have gone wrong with that. Howard McCord, a poet that I liked very much, has published twelve or fourteen books in the small-press field. He was a respected poet, a respected teacher, who arrived at a time when he felt that he was prepared for a selected poems, about a hundred-page book. I carried that book all over New York City, and I could not find anyone interested. There was the time when Doubleday took on Peter Wild, another small-press poet. Did they do a selected? No, they wanted a new book. The selected poems was done by New Rivers Press, another small press. I think that if we're going to have a successful symbiotic relationship, you might begin considering us as your farm league and give some basic support. For the $10,000 it might cost you to do a single book, I have existed for five years.

Vinz:

I'd agree with that.

Shoemaker:

One other thing about this collected poems that happened with Harcourt, Brace and World and has happened at least twice more since then: Philip Whalen, a poet of some substance and man of great sensitivity about typography, had beautiful books published for him in San Francisco by the Erewhon Society and by the Four Seasons Foundation and was lucky enough, when things weren't quite so tight, to get a contract for Harcourt, Brace and World for his collected poems. They did an atrocious job of book production, charged $17.50, so that if you were a smart buyer you could have wandered around bookstores in Berkeley and bought the original beautiful small-press editions for about the same money. Frank O'Hara's collected poems are $17.50, and that was always an art-book kind of price, but that seems to be the going price for collected volumes. And yet, I know that I can issue those books cheaper. I know that John Martin is issuing *The Loon,* a 408-page poem, for $6.00. I know that we can do it. I think our expectations have to be adjusted.

Vinz:

I would just add one thing. I, as a practice, give the poets 15 percent of the press run. They take the books with them, and then any money that comes in is theirs.

Zimmer:

I don't know about you, but my head is buzzing. I think we're very close to closing here. We've said a lot of things today. One more question. Ann Darr.

Ann Darr:

What was it that was said at this table, please, about poets taking their books with them? I could not hear what you said about that.

Zimmer:

Mark. She's asking you a question.

Vinz:

As a standard practice, a lot of small presses can't pay royalties. For one thing, we just don't have the bookkeeping to do so, so a lot of small presses simply give the author a percentage of the press run, and that way the author can take them and sell them and make probably more money that way.

Darr:

I do not publish with a small press but with a large trade press, and in my contract it says I may not do that. And I've so far gone along with them and never taken books myself to my own readings. Well, if the people who put the reading on care enough, they've gotten them from the publisher months in advance, and it takes that kind of preparation. If they haven't, there are no books around.

Halpern:

But Ann, can't you—you can buy your books at your author's discount and then sell them, no? Is that in the contract?

Darr:

It's in the contract that I may not sell my own books, and I've gotten to the point where I've carried around a suitcase myself, because when I found out that that's how books were sold, that a book salesman takes a suitcase, exactly as they did in 1889, and goes into each bookstore and plumps it down, and the book salesman can't read. . . .

Randall:

That's one difference between the commercial presses and the small presses.

Shoemaker:

If I were you I would get myself a resale number for tax purposes and an open account at your publisher and buy them. They cannot then forbid you from selling them. Buy them as a bookstore. I think it's ludicrous, maybe another example of the archaic method of distribution, if that's built into your contract and others.

Zimmer:

It's a curious contract you have, it really is. I remember a meeting of university presses, as a matter of fact, and there was a meeting of sales people, and they were talking about the poets on their lists, and they were all agreeing that they were a bunch of nuts, and one said, "Yes, as a matter of fact, we have one poet who just comes in and buys his book by the barrel-load and just carries it out. He's the best customer for the book." And he thought it was awful, you know, that a poet would do something like this. We love them. We love them. Yes?

Shoemaker:

I just wanted to ask, you were the one to raise the point of whether the commercial presses might not feed money into small presses. I wonder if the university presses as a system have thought about small presses in residence on campuses under your wing? I know of one instance where it has happened very successfully, and it's a method of teaching both design and bookmaking and having a small press with some small subsidy on campus.

Zimmer:

That's certainly something to consider. Yes.

Halpern:

I'm curious as to what will happen with the idea of that national poetry series. I mean does it mean that the whole thing has been outlined—and you might say that's a good idea—and then that's the end of it? Or does it mean that somebody's going to have to take charge and do it? I mean, no one's got their hand up about taking over here.

Zimmer:

Has anybody got their hand up? Yes, Galen Williams.

Williams:

Do you know about the Associated Writers Program that has awarded a poetry prize?

Halpern:

A poetry prize?

Williams:

They've set up judges and they've—do you know what I'm talking about? But anyway, the chairman of that has tried to get other university presses to take some of the people who were recommended at high levels, as Stanley mentioned, this idea of sharing—

Zimmer:

As a matter of fact, he sent letters around to university presses, I believe, asking if there are university presses willing to represent some selections from this group of manuscripts.

Audience:

About five have agreed to do that.

Zimmer:

Is that right? Five have agreed. That's similar to what you were proposing, as a matter of fact.

Halpern:

Yes, I haven't heard about it. It was just an idea to get five more books published a year, if you believe that there are five books out there that ought to be published that won't be published next year. But maybe people, in the end, don't really believe that. I don't know.

Zimmer:

I believe it. I believe it.

Audience:

There are a lot more than that.

Halpern:

Well, I was being modest. It was a modest estimate.

Audience:

Dan, I will tell you what will happen.

Halpern:

You want to take it over?

Audience:

You'll have an impeccable jury, a superb Librarian of Congress and Consultant in Poetry, and one manuscript is going to be head and shoulders above anything else that is submitted. It will be by Ezra Pound Hoover and will consist of character sketches, very mordant—along the lines of Martial—of all the leading members of Congress.

Zimmer:

Did we get that on tape? Anyone else want to address Dan on this? He's going to go away disappointed, I think.

Halpern:

I'm not disappointed, I have my series. I mean, you know, I'm just thinking of a possibility of getting more books published.

Zimmer:

Yes, absolutely. Okay, thank you very much, and God bless you all.

Publication in Magazines

E. V. Griffith, chairman; Alan Austin; Robert Boyers; Larry McMurtry; Theodore Solotàroff; Ramona Weeks; David Young

Kunitz:

I'm glad we have some survivors for the second day of the conference.

The panel this morning consists of representatives of a varied assortment of magazines, little and not so little. The chairman of the panel, whom I'm introducing now, is E. V. Griffith. According to the official biography, he was born in northern Minnesota, has lived most of his life in California—the North Coast —graduated from the University of Minnesota, where he edited the campus literary magazine, and then returned to California, where he became manager of a commercial printing firm. He then published a little magazine with the rather somber title *Hearse,* which he edited beginning 1957 and then buried it in 1961 but then had a second series later. Currently he's editing Poetry *NOW,* which I earnestly recommend to you, those of you who don't know it. It's a tabloid presentation of poetry, and it's edited with really beautiful taste. It is an exciting publication in every respect. Mr. Griffith will introduce his own panelists. Here he is.

E. V. Griffith:

Good morning. We're going to be speaking about the publication of poetry and fiction in magazines. The members of our panel from whom you will be hearing individually, after some opening remarks by myself, are David Young, who edits *Field* magazine; next to him, Robert Boyers of *Salmagundi* magazine; Larry McMurtry, a novelist; Ramona Weeks of *Inscape* magazine; Ted Solotaroff of the *American Review;* and Alan Austin of *Black Box* magazine. You'll be hearing from them in due course.

America today probably has more writers than at any time in her history. A new "official" crop is being churned out each year by the score and more of creative writing programs at colleges and universities across the country. The graduates of these programs then enter upon their new roles as poet, short-story writer, fiction writer—officially chartered by academia and armed with an M.F.A. degree as proof of their new status as writers in the world at large.

There are also at the present time probably more magazines than at any time in America's history. *The Reader's Guide to Periodical Literature,* a standard piece of library impedimenta, indexes several hundred "commercial" titles, and *The Directory of Little Magazines,* which is restricted to little magazines and journals, indexes more than one thousand little magazines. And there are, of course, magazines that appear in neither of these two directories. We'll be talking, as I said, about the publication of poetry and fiction in magazines, since magazines are not only a vehicle for the publication of fiction but also a proving ground for the permanent literature of tomorrow which often appears in magazines and then goes on to appear in books.

To define our parameters, there are various types of magazines that are publication sources for fiction and poetry. There are first the little magazines, which are called "little" primarily because their audiences are small, but these have a great reputation as the discoverers of literature and as a showcase for much talent that ultimately goes on to importance.

In the 1920s, when little magazines began to attract serious attention in this country, there were probably not more than fifty such magazines in the entire country. This is quite a small number, of course, compared to the one thousand that are being published today. The little magazines, which many of you will have seen, range from handsome letterpress publications on fine quality paper to publications printed by offset or by mimeograph. Most of them are center-stapled or side-stapled, and have fewer than one hundred pages or so per issue. The little magazines are named everything imaginable—from *Abraxas* to *Vagabond,* from the *Chowder Review* to *Yellow Brick Road.* The circulation of most of these little magazines is in the low hundreds. Almost none of them has as many as three thousand or four thousand readers.

The content of the little magazine is extremely varied—stories, poems, graphics, manifestos—and it ranges in quality from excellent to awful. The little is a training ground for new talent, but it is also a burial ground for the talent that never makes it beyond the parameters of the little magazine. But the influence of the magazines is truly enormous, and, although it's an influence that's not often felt until decades after the work has actually appeared, before the writer goes on to make a reputation, you eventually look back in retrospect at the little magazines and see that they truly were the training ground for important talent. One survey of little magazines, done a few years ago, indicates that over 80 percent of the major names of literature of the twentieth century first published in little magazines. These are people like Sherwood Anderson, Hemingway, Eliot, Carl Sandburg, Frost, Marianne Moore, and dozens of others.

A close ally to the so-called true little magazine is, of course, the literary journal, which is published quarterly, usually but not always with some type of university or college affiliation. The literary journals are many and varied. They include publications like *Antaeus*, the *Antioch Review*, the *California Quarterly*, the *Chicago Review*, *Epoch*, *Field*, the *Hudson Review*, the *Iowa Review*, *New Letters*, *Northwest Review*, the *Paris Review*, the *Partisan Review*, *Salmagundi*, *Shenandoah*, the *Sewanee Review*, the *Southern Review*, *Tri-Quarterly*, and there are many more. The literary magazine and journal usually tends to be more conservative and establishment-oriented than the more rambunctious, experimental little magazine. A literary review, in a typical issue, will carry maybe a half-dozen articles and/or book reviews. Interviews with writers are also popular features of such magazines. Few literary magazines carry more than a couple of short stories per issue, if any, and this is an indication of the rather limited market for short fiction in today's magazine world, which we'll be discussing in the course of our panel.

There are at least three other types of literary publications that should probably be mentioned in terms of defining our territory: there are poetry tabloids, such as *American Poetry Review, Invisible City*, and my own magazine, *Poetry NOW*; there is the magazine that is actually a book, which many of you know, such as *American Review*, which appears as a mass-produced paperback; and there is at least one audio magazine—*Black Box*—which is presented on two cassette tapes in a pasteboard slipcase.

One of the major aspects of little magazines that should not go unmentioned is that it is relatively easy to start a little magazine; it is much more difficult to keep one going. The ephemeral nature of little magazines is one thing that characterizes them. The failure of the little can occur from two major reasons: the slow bankrupting of the editor to support publication costs and the disappointment that comes to many editors who start out a magazine with a "mission" and then find that nobody is really paying much attention to their mission.

The embryo editor of a little magazine—and this is less true of the literary magazine, since many literary magazines have university support or other more stabilized funding than the true little magazines—is often blissfully unmindful of printing costs and the problems of distribution. Many editors start out, as I said, with a mission. They don't want to make money. They want to reform the world. They want to discover genius. They want to publish great literature. Few find an immediate or very enthusiastic audience. One of the horrors of publishing a little magazine, I think, is the editor who publishes a magazine into what seems to be a vacuum—you gather material, you publish a magazine, two hundred or three hundred copies, five hundred copies, you have immediate distribution problems. You mail a few copies around, and you may get some letters back from the contributors to your magazine saying, "I got the issue"—this type of thing. But from the world at large, there's very often kind of a dead silence. A few subscriptions trickle in and then—panic!—they stop. You get no more subscriptions for a time, and, in the meantime, the type for your second issue of your little magazine is being set, and the grocer is demanding his due.

At this point, some editors of little magazines simply stop publication. The second issue never appears, or, if it does, the third issue does not. So exit a magazine and an editor, this again testifying to the ephemeral nature of the little magazine. But enter stage right a bright new young man or woman who will tell you, "I'm going to start a magazine."

Some of the little magazines and literary journals manage to stay afloat for a long period of time. But long life does not a large circulation make. Of the poetry journals, for example, Poetry (Chicago), launched by Harriet Monroe in 1912, will soon have been in continuous print for sixty-three years, as a monthly, and not having missed a single issue in its sixty-three years. Yet Poetry, after that long a lifetime, has never managed a circulation of greater than eleven thousand—present circulation is in the nine thousand range. Some of the other literary journals have also been around for a long period of time. Paris Review, for example, recently published its sixty-third issue; the Partisan Review and the Hudson Review have also been around for more than a couple of decades. These, again, have not achieved large readerships. The readerships of these magazines are substantially less, in most instances, substantially less than ten thousand copies per issue.

Some of the "independent" little magazines, as contrasted to the literary magazines, have also been around for a long period of time, and these are supported mainly by their handful of subscribers and by the financial indulgences of their editors. One poetry magazine—this has been around for a considerable period—is George Hitchcock's Kayak magazine, which is now at its fortieth issue; it has a circulation of only twelve hundred copies. Another lesser-known but long-lived poetry magazine, Marvin Malone's Wormwood Review, has recently published its sixtieth issue, and it has kept its circulation deliberately at seven hundred copies and never tried to go beyond seven hundred copies.

To continue to publish a little magazine, or a literary magazine—and the focus today is the contents of the magazine rather than the magazines themselves as being a major outlet for the publication of poetry and fiction—to continue to publish a magazine, since it's almost always a losing proposition, demands deep dedication and almost inflexible purpose. There are plenty of both around, and both among editors of little magazines and literary journals. James Boatwright, who edits a magazine called *Shenandoah,* might well be speaking for a score of other editors when he expressed it in this manner:

I believe in diversity, pluralism, and more choices and more options, for reader and writer. Everything in the economics of commercial publishing militates against diversity: huge corporations swallow up one publishing house after another, newspapers disappear faster than you can keep track. Noncommercial publishing may be the only chance we will have for difference, decentralization, for the quirky, odd, and determinedly individualistic.

With the considerable number of magazines that are in print today it should follow—and usually does—that a new author worth his salt can manage to get published. Admittedly, his audience in the little magazines and the literary magazines may be a very limited one, but his work can at least see print, and he can know that he has at least some readers.

For the would-be poet, there are literally scores of little magazines devoted exclusively to poetry. Some of these—*Poetry NOW* (my own), *Poetry, American Poetry Review, Poetry Northwest*—have fairly substantial reputations (in the case of my own publication, thank God), and the writer of poetry has these and many other lesser-known outlets available to him. The writer of literary criticism and book reviews finds potential readership in a number of the literary journals as sources of publication or in a biannual such as *Parnassus,* which is devoted exclusively to book reviews and to literary appreciations—an excellent magazine. However, the publication of fiction in magazines has fallen on lean days. There are only one or two magazines in the United States devoted exclusively to the publication of fiction, although a number of the literary quarterlies will occasionally do a "Special All-Fiction Number."

It remains the better-grade commercial magazines that appear to be publishing the highest percentage of quality fiction in the country today—an opinion some of my colleagues may disagree with. If the annual 0. Henry Awards are any type of indicator—and this may be a loose indicator at best—in the 1975 volume of *The O. Henry Prize Stories,* of the eighteen stories included in that volume, three are from the *Atlantic,* three from the *New*

Yorker, and two from *Esquire,* with one each from *Harper's, Mademoiselle,* and *Redbook,* all of which are commercial magazines. The literary magazines supply the remaining six stories: two each from *Antaeus* and *Shenandoah* and one each from *Fiction* and *Greensboro Review.* The other annual compendium of short stories, *The Best American Short Stories* collection, tends to generally reprint more from literary magazines than the *Prize Stories* collection does.

The same commercial magazines that are the major publishers of quality magazine fiction—magazines like *Harper's,* the *Atlantic,* the *New Yorker*—are also three of the major outlets for quality poetry in magazines, although combined, these magazines probably do not publish more than 150 poems a year. They also tend to be probably more receptive to the established poetry and fiction writer than they are to the newcomer. That, too, is debatable, depending on one's perception. The *Nation,* the *New Republic,* and *Esquire* are some other "prestige" markets for poetry. The flashier, fleshier magazines—such commercial magazines as *Playboy* and *Penthouse,* that type of thing—ignore poetry almost entirely, although they do publish some worthwhile fiction.

The publication in little magazines and literary journals can help an author gain an audience, can help him build a reputation. It cannot earn him much of a living, since almost none of the noncommerical magazines can afford to pay their writers, or if they do pay them it is a very token payment. In most instances, the little magazines and many of the literary publications can afford only to give their authors contributor's copies. That again is not much of a way to make a living.

With those opening remarks, we will hear from the members of our panel who will discuss their own perceptions of the publication of poetry and fiction in magazines today and, as regards publication in magazines, will perhaps make some broader comments on what they consider to be the "state of health" of poetry and magazine fiction in America today. Are there areas of significant change or experimentation ahead? Does an expanded audience for poetry and fiction truly exist, and if so, what can be done by today's magazines to reach this audience? We will hear in rotation from the members of our panel. First we will hear from David Young, the editor of *Field* magazine.

David Young:

I think it might help if I just talked very briefly about how *Field* got started and what aims it had; then I will go on to talk about how things are now, what sorts of problems we perceive; and then I will just very briefly try to address myself to those last three questions that E. V. Griffith threw out for us.

I guess I came of age as a writer myself in the sixties, the early sixties, and there were, I think, about three poetry magazines then that I used to look forward to seeing with a good deal of anticipation. One was Robert Bly's magazine, which was first the *Fifties,* then the *Sixties,* and now the *Seventies;* one was John Logan's *Choice*; and one was George Hitchcock's *Kayak.* I was also a pretty faithful reader in those days of a magazine called the *Carleton Miscellany.* Around 1969, which was when we started *Field,* one primary impulse was simply a sense of absence. Bly's magazine came out so irregularly that it began to look as though there'd be one issue per decade, so looking forward to that was rather tedious business. *Choice,* too, appeared so irregularly and was often so hard to get hold of that one couldn't count on that. And for me, at any rate, *Kayak* had begun to be a little bit too much of the same kind of thing, and I realized that I didn't have the same sense of anticipation when a new issue was due.

So our aim was in a way really quite simple: we wanted to try to create a literary magazine, a poetry journal that would be quite readable. I am not going to mention negative examples, but I think everybody has had the experience of picking up a magazine devoted exclusively, or almost exclusively, to poetry and finding that they simply couldn't make their way through it. And I think we also wanted to try to create a magazine that wasn't quite so eccentric as something like the *Fifties* or *Sixties,* which was so stamped or marked by its editor's personal biases. We wanted, I guess in a way, to combine the virtues of the two categories that E.V. Griffith has defined as the "little mag" and the "literary journal."

We had a couple of other smaller aims: we wanted a magazine that would come out on time, and I'm proud to say that that's been the case with *Field* right along. Twice a year it's appeared on schedule. Its going to be about a week late this fall, and we're all wringing our hands about that. Also, we wanted to run a magazine that wouldn't have any backlog. I think one of the most irritating things that authors experience is having a poem, or story, or essay accepted and then waiting, say, two years to see it come out, because the magazine has developed a large backlog of accepted material. We've been able to hold up to that aim. We also wanted to pay our contributors. It seemed to us that although no one could make a living or get rich off their poetry, there was a kind of self-respect and professionalism connected with being able to pay contributors that we wanted to emulate. We also decided to work with a group of editors, and that's been the case right along. There have always been four or five editors who are in on the final selection of material. This is partly just a matter of trying to share the work, trying to create a magazine that wasn't simply one person's taste and that, therefore, was a little more catholic, and also just to share the responsibility. I think it's very difficult if you're an editor and you're solely responsible for what does or does not get printed. Then the pressure on you, through friendships and sort of implied reciprocities, and so forth, gets pretty intense. And we simply felt we would find it easier to make the tough decisions if we did it as a group, because we were particularly determined not to print work that we could not stand by, that we did not feel was really superior. And, of course, that has meant right along offending people—I'll get to that in a little more detail in a moment, or maybe we'll get to it in the question period. I don't know.

In practice, we have quite a significant volume of contributions now. I would guess, on a low month, somewhere around two thousand poems come to us. On a busy month it's more like three thousand. To deal with that volume we have a system whereby two editors read everything that comes in, and we rotate this responsibility. They then decide what material the entire editorial board should consider, and we meet about twice a month. At those sessions we read the poems aloud and discuss them in detail and vote on whether or not they'll go in. It's a fairly intensive process, and when a poem has stood up to that kind of scrutiny, then we can usually feel pretty good about having it in the magazine. I would guess that, if you're interested again, the statistics of the material that is submitted—what gets looked at, read, considered, discussed in detail in those sessions that involve all the editors—is something like 15 to 20 percent of what is submitted to us.

I think literary magazine editors want, especially when starting out, to think that they can edit in the fullest sense of the term, which means, if possible, helping writers. In practice that's a rather tricky business. There are some writers who are anxious to hear in detail what kind of reaction you have to their work, and there are others who would rather not know, and it's very often difficult to tell who's who. Sometimes people profess an interest and they don't really feel it; sometimes writers who seem as though they might be offended are in fact grateful for some kind of detailed response. When we can, when it seems practical, we often try to suggest that poems be improved or changed. We often ask to see them again if our suggestions seem reasonable to the author, but it's really hard to categorize the way that this goes on. But again, having a number of editors makes the job of trying to help authors by particular response and by some help in editing a little easier.

I thought, too, I should mention the question of solicitation. Right from the start we found that depending simply on the flow of unsolicited contributions would not bring us the material we were hoping to get. So we do quite a bit of soliciting and with happy results most of the time. I would guess that in a given issue of the magazine something like 60 to 70 percent of the printed material is material that has come because someone has written a note to someone asking for new work. But, of course, the other side of that is that since we do not print work because of somebody's reputation or because somebody is a friend or even because we have asked to see material, we often get angry letters or lose friends or whatever. In other words, I suppose the list of people rejected is probably as distinguished as the list of people accepted, and, I think, established poets often get to feeling that nobody really ought to presume to solicit work from them and then turn around and reject it if they are merely a little magazine. And this has made things rather difficult and delicate at times.

I don't think I'll say much about cost, because everybody here knows that costs have risen. Our magazine cost $1.50 when we started in 1969. Two years ago it went up to $1.75, now it costs $2.00. We regret that, but at the same time I think that the people who want to subscribe to it or buy it in a bookstore are willing to pay that.

I think we were quite sanguine at the beginning about distribution in a little bit the way that E.V. has described people when they start a magazine: it will find its audience if it's good enough, we don't need to worry about that. To a certain extent that's true; that is, I think good magazines do find their way into the hands of people who need them and want to read them. We've become more and more aware that we are not reaching as many people as we need to, that we have got to increase our distribution. We're trying various ways to solve this problem. I can't say really that it has been solved, so I'll be interested in today's question period, if there's any exchange of information about this matter. What we're doing, the most recent thing we're doing is trying to get the magazine used more in college classrooms, where we feel it really could serve a purpose. To that end we have stuck our necks out financially and rented a booth at the next MLA convention. We'll try to get several other magazines to go in with us and see if we can get our product noticed by those university and college teachers who attend the convention.

I think I'll stop there and wait for the question period to elaborate on any of the things that I've said or things that I haven't said that you want to ask about.

Robert Boyers:

I'm Robert Boyers of *Salmagundi* magazine. The magazine that I edit, for those of you who don't know it, is a quarterly of the

humanities and social sciences. As such, it is not devoted exclusively
to the publication of creative literature—poetry, and fiction, and
drama. It does devote a considerable amount of space in most issues to the publication of some poems, occasional stories, and occasionally even full-length plays. The interest of the magazine,
though, is, I suppose, primarily in the area of cultural criticism,
and it is from that perspective that I come to this meeting and
that I am interested in addressing the question of the health of
poetry and fiction. So you'll forgive me if my remarks seem somewhat oblique to the issues as they have been raised in a straight-
forward way by other panelists.

My sense, in general, is that the culture is both healthy and
unhealthy with respect to the publication of poetry and fiction. I'll
be quite precise about this. There is a state of health in the sense
that it is possible for almost anybody, regardless of talent or training or background, to publish almost anything in a variety of different places and to feel some degree of satisfaction in having
managed to get his stuff in print. I suppose that that is healthy if
one thinks of health in therapeutic terms as being good for people's egos and for the sense that they ought to continue to keep
writing and trying. And I suppose, in a sense, I do think that's
health.

The culture is, however, it seems to me, singularly unhealthy in
its encouragement of a kind of cultural pluralism which insists,
for example, that the federal government grant funds to support
almost anything, almost any kind of enterprise, and that various
publishing groups, conglomerates, and so on, together use money
to support altogether unworthy operations and enterprises. That
seems to me to be a very confusing situation which one can trace
to the influence of the poets themselves. The poets, many of them,
of course, teaching in colleges and universities around the country, have been assiduous, it seems to me, to cultivate a sense of
what they do in terms of immediacy, nakedness, glibness and so
on, at the expense of craft, discrimination, and the capacity to
read critically. Students in poetry-writing courses, for example, in
the college from which I come, regularly enter these writing
workshops with no capacity to read a poem and are encouraged
by poets who teach these courses to express themselves in chaotic
ways without ever having undergone elementary procedures. At
the same time, of course, the colleges and universities themselves
regularly grant credit towards degrees for taking these courses in
self-expression, which really seem to me to have very little value
and to produce very few writers of merit, whatever the school one
happens to be teaching at.

Of course, this situation produces a variety of cultural spin-offs.
One of them, for example, goes by the name of *American Poetry*

Review, a magazine that I myself write for, which I don't feel myself too proud to resist writing for, but which nevertheless, I think, might stand as symptomatic of the situation I am trying to describe. This is a magazine which, as most of you know, attempts to print a variety of poems, articles, interviews, occasional stories in fact, but which has to any careful observer—I suppose even to any random observer—absolutely no editorial view, no editorial taste to speak of. In this magazine it is possible to find on page 1 an entirely meaningless and obscure poem, written by someone who does not have the first notion of how to construct a stanza of verse, and published in the same issue on page 45 are two poems by David Wagoner which are singularly beautiful and well crafted. What is one to make of this? Well, if one is a professional, if one has taken a consistent interest in the life of poetry and fiction in our own time, I suppose one learns to read selectively and to look around in magazines like *American Poetry Review* and find what is vital and interesting. But if one has not been trained professionally to read critically, then one is likely to be very confused. It seems to me that if we're going to address the state of the literary arts in America we have to address singularly the question of this confusion.

Now, one of the places we could begin, I think, to address the confusion is in the matter of literature as politics or literature as fad. It seems to me, for example, that the interest in native American poetry—and for that matter most of the interest in black poetry—in this country has nothing really to do with poetry at all. These seem to me to be political and cultural phenomena of another sort which occasionally, and only incidentally, bear on the state of literature in general. And it seems to be very confusing to talk about the publication of poetry and the audience available for good poems and stores in terms of the audience that reads the stuff coming out of the Broadside Press. The kids who read stuff from the Broadside Press, at my college for example, do not know how to read poems for the most part, have absolutely no use (so they say) for the poems of Wallace Stevens (or Stanley Kunitz for that matter), and still continue to think—and are encouraged in this by their professors—that what they're reading is verse and what they're cultivating is a feeling for creative literature. This seems to me a great mistake. My own feeling is that if, as a community of literate people, we are interested in improving the level of literacy in the culture, what we ought to do for a start is to stop making a fetish out of the creation of poetry and fiction. Those of us who are interested in serious poetry and fiction will read it, will study it, will try to perpetuate it, and will reach other people like ourselves who have this interest. At the same time, I think we ought to be encouraging students and young people who don't know what they want to cultivate an interest in consecutive argumentation, rational argument, an interest in ideas, in public issues, in politics of a serious nonapocalyptic sort, and to stop telling them that the way to become cultured and educated is to read the poetry coming out of the Broadside Press.

Well, I suppose we can go on from there in the question and answer period. Obviously, as you see, my remarks have been very oblique but hopefully provocative anyway.

Larry McMurtry:

That is a hard act to follow. Looking around, both at the panel and at the audience, I have somewhat the sense that I've got myself caught in a room full of poets and I'm not sure how much interest anyone is going to have in anything said about fiction.

I am a novelist. I've always been a novelist. I've been publishing novels for about eighteen years and I've met and known and talked with an awful lot of other novelists and short-story writers around America. I've hardly met a one, in all the time I've been going around, that is really very appreciative of the situation in magazine publishing in regard to fiction.

Now for decades, the little magazines have done a magnificent job with poetry; the quarterlies, obviously, have done a good job with criticism; and the slick magazines and commercial magazines have done an excellent job with journalism. But I don't think that American magazines have done much with fiction at all. And I believe we are just now in a period in which we're really witnessing the death of a form—namely, the short story—simply because there is really no place, or very few places, in which quality short stories can be published satisfactorily.

I taught writing for a number of years formally at universities, and I, in a broad sense, still teach it informally. I have a bookshop here in the city, and I suppose that I receive something like 100, 150 longish manuscripts a year just off the street. They just walk in the door, young people seeking advice, asking for someone to tell them someplace to go with their manuscripts. And if they're short-story writers, if they are novelists, or are trying to be, struggling to be novelists, I can be of some assistance to them because I know a lot of editors and I can send them around to these editors in the hope that something that they write will engage one or another of the editors to the point where he or she would like to work with them. They might, thus, receive a certain amount of encouragement, and might go on to develop as fiction writers.

For the short story I can't really do that. I think just within the last fifteen or twenty years we have seen the short story atrophy. It was, as you know, quite common. The important fiction writers of the twenties and thirties grew up more or less ambidextrously in terms of the long form and the short form. Faulkner and Fitzgerald and Hemingway were just as good at short fiction as they were at long fiction. A few writers struggled on—were able to struggle on—with this perhaps even into the fifties. Philip Roth began as a short-story writer and became a novelist, but I don't believe that he or anyone else in that generation is really practicing the two forms with very much success. Speaking from my generation of fiction writers in America, I can only think of two: Donald Barthelme, who is going to read here tonight, and, I suppose, Leonard Michaels. They have developed principally as short-story writers and managed to achieve some reputation and sustain some kind of a career simply because there are no places to publish what they write, and if they go to the quarterlies, or if they go to the little magazines, they might occasionally be published, but they cannot survive financially. This situation has never bothered me personally, because I never really tried to write short fiction. I seemed to have found out right away that I was more comfortable with longer forms, and almost all of my publication in magazines—I have published between twenty and twenty-five essays—have originated as suggestions with editors. That is, I am not self-motivated to the short form at all. I have had, I believe, three excerpts from my six novels published in magazines. That has not been satisfactory either. In fact, I have begun to discourage my agent even from trying to publish excerpts because the excerpting of fiction is a strange, rather odd practice in which generally the chapter that's excerpted is the chapter that is least intrinsic to the material of the novel; for example, I just did it with a novel that I have just published, in fact, today. I had a chapter published in *Playboy* this summer, and it was the one chapter in the novel that was totally excerptable. It was just kind of a black humorist extravaganza. It was easily pulled out, but I would hate for the readers who read it to follow it to the novel expecting to find the rest of the novel to be more or less like this chapter. I think that's common and rather standard. When editors look for something to pull out of a novel, they find the least organic, the least tightly worked-in chapter, and there you are.

So, at the moment I will leave it at that and pass on to the other panelists, but I don't think that the situation in magazine publishing in regard to fiction is at all healthy or appealing just now.

Ramona Weeks:

I'm going to talk basically about the thing I know best, which is our magazine, *Inscape,* which may be of particular interest because it is a magazine that failed ten years ago and then came back to life for a number of reasons. I think it provides a case in point of "the little magazine that could." It started as a handsome four-page quarterly in Albuquerque in 1959. The founding editors were E.W. Tedlock, Jr., who was D.H. Lawrence scholar at the University of New Mexico—he now has his own press, the San Marcos Press; the second founders were Joe Ferguson, Jr., Elaine Busch Kalmar, and myself. All of us were associated in some way with the University of New Mexico, and we, in our infinite wisdom, considered ourselves inheritors of Spud Johnson-Witter Bynner-Taos-Suckegg Newell School of Little Magazines. We thought we were following in the steps of a great tradition.

We wanted to publish good poetry in our area, New Mexico, that we felt was not being published. I worked for the University of New Mexico Press as an editor. I read manuscripts for the *New Mexico Quarterly*. I saw that we were turning down a lot of poems, good poems, that I felt should be published. All of us had friends who were poets, and we thought good poets: Robert Creeley, Keith Wilson, Charles Tomlinson, Malcolm Bradbury, A. Alvarez, and Scott Momaday. And you've got to remember that, although some of those names are fairly well known now, in 1959 and 1960 they weren't. Tedlock was head of the committee that distributed the D.H. Lawrence fellowships and had access to a number of poets who applied for those fellowships and came there. Most of us were poets, Ferguson and I perhaps wrote poetry most steadily, and Tedlock wrote occasional poems.

In putting out the magazine we had the help of a superb graphic designer named Roland Dickey, and he set up the most beautiful, superb, clean-looking layout that you have ever seen. And we had access to a printer who wasn't going to soak us for a lot of money. It was the UNM printing plant, and I'm sure the UNM printing plant gave us a good price because of our university connections, because I knew them and worked with them. Although this wasn't a university publication, it had sort of an association, because we were there; and the English Department gave us some money toward publication, and various people of the faculty contributed. So it had a quasi-university status.

We also had someone eager to do the recordkeeping and all the book work, and the "scut work," as I call it—the mailing and the billing, the subscriptions and the correspondence. This was our bright housewife with four kids, who was an English major who went on, some years later, to get her doctorate.

We had a bit of money, a grant or so from the English Department, as I said, and we got about fifty subscribers. The *New Mexico Quarterly* let us use a set of labels to send sample copies to university libraries, and most of those subscribed. We charged very little; I think we charged $2 a year, and we put out four issues. The rest of it was, you know, a little money here—I think Elaine Kalmar bought her own stamps, Joe Ferguson and I bought some office supplies, and paid for the printing of stationery and some rejection slips. Tedlock persuaded poets Winfield Townley Scott, Witter Bynner, etc., to donate some dollars and to tell their friends to subscribe. We didn't need a lot of money. We published 250 to 300 copies. Our average cost per issue was about $75. I think the first letterpress issue cost $60; this was a very handsome, clean-looking letterpress.

The first issue was a typewriter offset number which I thought just looked terrible, so we jettisoned that in favor of our professional graphic-designed job. Postage at that time was five cents, I think, and so we could mail our issue for ten cents, and things have changed considerably since that time. So I thought we had all the ingredients: the desire to put out a magazine, the poets, the contacts with printers, backers, a designer, someone to do all the hard bookkeeping work without protest and without pay, a few pesos, and somebody who could tap people with pesos. And since we were friends, we all loved to get together once a month and drink wine and read the poems that had come in during the month, which we somehow managed to circulate. Our system was pretty—you know, we all had read the poems, generally there was a unanimous decision on a poem, but if one of us felt very strongly about a poem, the others said, "Okay. You can have it, if you really want it that badly." The process was painless, except that the money that trickled from friends and backers did slow, and in the course of human events, things happened. Our housewife was moving into another house, her fifth baby died of crib death. Tedlock declared himself tired of going hat-in-hand to people to beg for money. I entered a second marriage and quit my job and started writing some commercial things for money, and generally, we just decided to cut our losses and go our separate ways in 1960. We are still receiving requests, by the way, for issue 8 of *Inscape,* and for years I was writing back saying, "As soon as I find issue 8 of the first series, I'll send it to you." And then it occurred to me we never had an issue 8—7, that was our last issue.

So, ten years later, with some friends in Phoenix, we had a poetry-reading group. We started talking about starting a magazine in Arizona. There was no poetry magazine. There was—still is—the *Arizona Quarterly* from the University of Arizona. So, at any rate, we decided there needed to be an alternative, and somebody said, "I have a little money," and somebody said, "I have a little time, so why don't we revive *Inscape?*" We telephoned all the previous people and said, "Do you mind if we pick up the name?" And, of course, nobody minded. We published one issue in 1970, I believe, the first issue, when we heard, in a roundabout fashion, of another *Inscape* magazine being started. I contacted them and told them of our history, and so this periodical changed its name to the *Seneca Review* and said, "Why didn't you announce this in" wherever one announces things, *Directory of Little Magazines.* But anyway, we got to keep our name.

And the new *Inscape* was revived as part of a considerably more ambitious poetry-publishing program. The principal financial backer and coeditor Joy Harvey and I incorporated the Baleen Press to publish *Inscape* as a quarterly and to publish books of poetry. The books, by the way, constitute a strong list, reflecting our own interests in poets and in the region. The authors of our books, under the Baleen Press imprint, include Duane Niatum, who was born Duane McGinnis; J. D. Reed; Vern Rutsala; Ralph Mills, Jr.; Richard Shelton; W. A. Rucker; and a prison poet named Paul David Ashley, originally known as Charles Schmid; Diane di Prima, and several others. This reflects a regional bias which, in agreement with Mark Vinz yesterday, I agree is one of the functions of a press in a region that has a dearth of outlets and a plethora of poets.

Back to the magazine, which itself is terribly behind schedule. We're up now to volume 4, number 4. If we had published four issues a year, we'd be at volume 6, number 3 or 4. And that tardiness is perhaps universal, I hope so. I'd hate to think we were the only ones who were behind schedule.

We have private lives outside the magazine. I have a job that brings an income, and *Inscape,* of course, does not produce any sort of income. All of us dislike those routines that are an inevitable part of producing a magazine, and we have more interesting things to do and to go to. We like to go to poetry readings, we like to write plays and poems of our own, and then we have a book that we are working on that we consider more interesting, perhaps. We used to round-robin read the manuscripts, three or four of us. Now Joy Harvey and I usually select the poems we like, we con an artist into illustrating the issue for love or for money, and we pay him if we have to. I think the graphic excellence of our magazine is one of the reasons it has been well received. People are not buying just a collection of fifteen or twenty poems; they're also buying a really splendidly produced work of art. And I think that has broadened our audience and our subscription list.

The way we work is that each of us or one of our associates will take over an issue, will solicit the poetry sometimes, read it, handle all the details from the selection of type, the proofreading, the

choice of paper, the paper cover material, and the liaison with the
poets and the printer. We occasionally bring in a guest editor, as
we did recently with the Spanish-English issue. We asked a couple
of people to recommend someone competent to edit a periodical
like this. They recommended Leroy Quintana. And we had a
Peruvian teacher friend in Phoenix who spoke Spanish very thoroughly and who, incidentally, found herself correcting the Spanish from some of the southwestern Spanish poets who weren't
quite sure of their grammar and their accents even though they
had grown up speaking it. The result was absolutely beautiful,
even though it ended up costing $750.00 for 500 issues, which is
our usual press run. Since we sell the issues for $1.50 apiece,
we're not doing too well or we're losing money. And those are
only the costs I know about, and those do not include postage.

We're going to do a Chicago poets issue very shortly, and the editorial work on it is being done by Ralph Mills, Jr. A new poets
issue is coming out soon. We've had great success with doing special issues because we find a number of libraries will write and
request: "We're interested in your issue on Spanish-English poets," or
"We're interested in your issue on the Chicago poets." Presently, all
the Chicago poets are now deluging us with poetry. I think they
think we're going to be doing issues from here on out on Chicago
poets. We'd like to do an issue on country-western lyrics. There are
many, many people in our area who write country-western lyrics,
and if we can find some good ones, I think we would be tempted
to do that. And also we are attempting to do a prison poets
issue that would grow out of some of the prison poets at the Arizona State Prison. I've mentioned one volume we're doing by
Charles Schmid. Unfortunately, Schmid was murdered this spring
by two of his inmate buddies, but he left a legacy of really fine
poetry. Another prison poet is named Michael F. X. Hogan—
Michael Francis Xavier Hogan—who won the P.E.N. Prize for a
prison poet this year. There's really quite a fund to choose from,
so we may be doing that.

We haven't explored doing an issue on concrete poetry, although if there's interest in this, we wouldn't be averse to doing
that. Nobody just sends anything to us. We might even devote an
issue to the work of one poet. Our prejudices, I think, would
exclude such things as haiku and cinquains. I think we'd run to
the nearest mousehole if somebody proposed an issue on that.
We're only prejudiced against things that make no sense to us,
that seem to us to have no organic unity as poems. We've published murderers, homosexuals, Vietnam veterans, Chicanos, Tex-
ans, blacks, Mormons, women, atheists. So I don't think we have
any real prejudices. I am sort of—this is a bias that's developed: I
don't like to publish the work of poets who start writing you one

month later about when is my poem going to appear in print. We had one lady who's fairly influential, I suppose. She reviews books of poetry for the *San Francisco Chronicle*. We accepted her poem, and she started sending us registered letters that we have to go to the mailbox and pay postage on half the time and pick up, saying: "When is my poem going to be in print?" So I think we finally suggested that she might be better off with someone with a more rapid publishing schedule. But most people are very generous and very tolerant and we love them.

About solicitation. We do solicit a lot of work. Rather, we let the word be known among people we've published before, people on university faculties that we know, that we're open to certain kinds of submissions. We took our name out of that *International Directory of Little Magazines,* et cetera, that Len Fulton puts out in Dustbooks, because we found that we were getting fifteen hundred poems a month from people who had not seen the magazine. So we hid ourselves under a listing, "The Baleen Press, publishes *Inscape,* not open to general submissions," which a lot of people complain about. But if they write to complain, I tell them that we will look at their manuscript. But I think that that gets rid of a lot of the dross and a lot of the garbage that comes in. They call us—somebody referred to us as elitist, and we're not trying to be that. We're just trying to manage with the resources we have. That's the only reason.

Because we are our own mistresses, more or less, we publish what we want; and that sort of freedom is exhilarating. We received one CCLM grant of $750, and I don't think we'll ever receive another one unless we furnish the required financial report, which we will do one of these days. It seems to me that the publication of an issue itself constitutes the proof of expenditure. We may apply for another grant. I understand the rules have changed now. We had a disaster with the grant. You had to raise money in your community to match this money. We decided to give a party and charge for drinks and sell an artist's work to raise money. We brought the artist from Louisiana at an expense of about $225. We collected money at the door. Somebody ripped off the $10 bill stack. We had the ones, the fives, and the twenties, but no tens at the end of the evening, so it really was a disaster. We prefer not to think about it, but I'm delighted the rules have changed. If we do apply for another grant and get it, we'll use the money to pay contributors or to promote the magazine in some fashion. We might send free copies to 250 university libraries.

We would like to arrange a Chicano poetry reading festival— that's one of our plans—in the community, to interest the community in what we're doing. And I think with the help of a number of groups, we can do that. The audience for poetry is growing, and there are more poets going out to the schools, to the elementary and secondary schools programs, more readings by poets in public places, even recognition of poets as cult heroes and cult heroines. And I think poets really can enlarge the audience for their works. I'm all for poets reading at civic centers, for brown-bag lunches. They have an obligation to do that kind of thing, to broaden their audience and appeal. When a poet goes in and buys the book of poetry at a bookstore, I don't think there's any reason why he cannot talk to the manager of that bookstore, not just about his own book, but about five or six others, and he can say, "Hey. People would be interested in this if you stocked it."

I think certain community groups ought to become more interested in poets in their community and more aware of them. I'm having a current controversy with the Association of American University Women, who is sponsoring an authors' luncheon, and there are little ladies who have published books with Dorrance or those where you pay. So I say those people really—having paid to publish themselves—are not authors. So I'm having a difficult time. I may just bag that.

I think poets have an obligation to boost the magazines they appear in. If they get two free issues, they ought to buy two or five more, send them to people, and say, "Hey, this is a good magazine. Why don't you subscribe?" Give poetry magazines for Christmas presents. I have a friend who does that, and it's very successful.

There are interesting little plans underfoot, I think, in our region to develop an audience for poetry. There's a group in Albuquerque I had a letter from recently, and I'll just read a couple of paragraphs from it, if I may:

Dear Ramona:

I have an idea for a southwest womens' poetry exchange. One of the problems of living and writing poetry in the Southwest is finding an audience. Wide spaces literally divide people who would really listen. It always feels good to have some response to your work. It also helps to know that other people have similar problems in the art. Perhaps the exchange would make us less insular.

The plan is for everyone on the enclosed mailing list to take one to six of her favorite unpublished poems, make twenty copies of each, and mail them to me. I will put them all together and mail a copy of everyone's work to you.

I think that's an interesting idea and has lots of potential, and we may even get an issue out of this kind of exchange. I'm looking forward to that.

I may as well say frankly that we publish *Inscape* as a great loss leader, I suppose, is the term. We don't make any money on it; we lose money on it. But we get some poetry volumes out of it. By the way, I have numbers of poets who write to me and say they'd like to publish a volume with us, and I say, "Our pages in the magazine are open." That's if we're not interested in considering his work at that time as a book. And I have a prejudice, I suppose, toward the poets who want you to publish their book, but don't want to necessarily be in your magazine because they're going to be in the *Paris Review* or the *Hudson Review* or *American Poetry Review*. And we use it sort of as a testing-ground, proving-ground, and to get good poems for the magazine.

Basically, I feel the editors who care about their magazines will get out the issues, and I think the allocation of dollars should be up to them. If I have the option of giving an artist a ream of wild strawberry paper or orange paper, and he'll illustrate an issue for me—and that's the kind of thing I do—we're really very freewheeling.

I think I'm going to stop there and you can ask questions if you want.

Theodore Solotaroff:

I'm the editor of *American Review*. I was going to talk a little bit about *American Review*, but—and maybe I will—what I'd rather do is address myself to some of the points that Mr. Boyers raised, which I think puts—well there's a Yiddish phrase for this, but we'll just say that it puts the issue on the table.

A lot of what he says I sort of agree with, though I am hampered from completely agreeing with him by a lot of experiences which began, I suppose, when I was a graduate student at the University of Chicago in the late fifties. As some of you may remember, Chicago was the home of the Chicago critics, the neo-Aristotelians, and there was no place in the country where rigorous, rational, coherent reading was not just encouraged but demanded. At the University of Chicago we were trained to read at about the rate of a page an hour, and I was a product of that process and proud of it. At the time I was also associated in a rather vague way with a magazine called the *Chicago Review* which I sort of did for rest and rehabilitation from my Aristotelian seminars.

And around 1957 the editorship changed, and a young man named Irving Rosenthal came in as editor. Irving was a rather strange young man, sort of a prototype for that typical U. of C. student known as Aristotle Schwartz, who may have had one foot in the great books but the other foot into all manner of intellectual dissipation and so on. He began to recruit writing that we had never seen at the press before, and one of the first things that he came around with was a rather ugly and obscene and vulgar story, I guess, about an operation in which the surgeon was using all manner of plumbing equipment for this operation. It was rather odious and poorly written, as we would have said in our seminars. Then there was a poem which was very long and kind of loosely Whitmanesque, I suppose, and very crude and didn't really have any particular visible craft to it. And it was all about some sort of generational poem, I guess, but it was hard to tell just what it was about. It was a very hysterical poem, so we thought. And then there was all manner of other writing that was coming out of more of what seemed to be the same place—namely, San Francisco—including some material from a novel by someone that we had heard of named Jack Kerouac, but this, too, seemed of the same ilk as that other stuff we were reading.

So there wasn't terribly much support for Irving, which was unfortunate because he needed it. The University of Chicago got wind of this special issue he was preparing to put together. They got wind of it through a Chicago columnist named Jack Mabley, who was carrying on the last vestiges of McCarthyism in Chicago and had been tipped-off that the *Chicago Review* was about to pollute the city of Chicago—which takes some doing—by this issue of this magazine which reached all of ninety-seven people in Hyde Park. So the president of the university sort of sicced the chairman of the humanities division on Irving Rosenthal and called him in and said, "Mr. Rosenthal, we really don't think that we want you to publish this material we've been hearing about"—they had asked to see it, of course. A couple of members of the English Department had read it and generally agreed with Jack Mabley, the columnist from the *Chicago Journal of America*. Anyway, this gets longer and longer, but, to cut matters short, they wouldn't let him publish this issue of the "little magazine." He could take maybe one of these items and drop it into this issue, and then another and drop it into the next issue, and another, and sort of sanitize it by associations.

He got very upset about it all and dropped out of school and went off to San Francisco. But before he left he formed a sort of temporary partnership with another young maverick around the university, and they took all this material and they put it into a magazine. They called this magazine *Big Table.* And when it turned out that the University of Chicago had been censoring and repressing, and what we ourselves—we high and mighty graduate students who were in touch with the happy few and the best that had been thought and said and all that—and what we were turning our backs on was a book called *Naked Lunch,* a poem called "Howl," a section of Kerouac's *The Subterraneans,* and assorted poems by the group of so-called San Francisco poets. What happened was that this issue became probably the most single important issue of a literary magazine since the postwar era because what it did was announce a whole new movement in American writing called the Beats.

So, that experience had a kind of cautionary effect on me, and when I got to be an editor I did try to remember that what might strike me, at least immediately, as not my taste and not up to my standards might five or ten years farther down the road turn out to be part of the literature of my country. So I really think that when you begin to apply standards of reason—and that's what criticism essentially is, applying a certain kind of rational discipline to the reading of imaginary works of art and discursive works, as we used to say at Chicago—when you do that, you oftentimes will get answers to questions that are your questions but are not questions that are being asked by the work itself. So it is probably as that Simon Suggs, a famous character out of nineteenth-century frontier literature, said, "It pays to be shifty in a new country." And literature is inevitably a new country. It is a new country every year; it's certainly a new country every decade, and you have to try to be as open as you can and to see around your own corners and to bend, but not bend so far that you crack.

Well, I don't know what this all has to do with *American Review,* except it represents the principles I edit the magazine wi·h, and that is that I try to look for material that leaves a scar, even though that scar may not be very pleasant. Scars usually aren't. Maybe the word is wound. Material that doesn't simply confirm my own taste of what is good and what is true and what is beautiful, but rather begins to stretch my mind a bit and make me think, "Gee, this is a very strange and sort of adversary experience, but boy I can't get this thing out of my mind."

To put this sort of plea for a certain kind of breadth into context, it also happens that we're living in a society which educates about half of its younger population—sends them to college. I think that up until World War II we would send, at most, about 8 percent of each generation to college, and now we send over 50. And that means that a lot of people begin to have access to literary education who would never have had it before, certainly whose families never had it before. And some of those who have this access actually begin to hang around that stuff called poems and stories and plays and even to try their hand at writing it. They also have things like creative writing programs now which they never had before, and you can get degrees in it and so on. So the society has begun to foster a whole new sort of literary pluralism—a phrase used before—and a much more diverse and populous kind of literary community, not only of readers but also of writers. And there is not much you can do about it.

You can say literature really is for only three hundred people in the society who are able to read at the very height of the great intellectual traditions of the West. But it doesn't work that way. It doesn't really work that way in America, where we've always had a kind of crazy, mixed-up, democratic literary community anyway. Try to think of Mark Twain as a French writer, much less a German one. I don't think that I'm vulgarizing my own argument. I am just trying to say that Walt Whitman was not what one would call a traditional nineteenth-century poet, even of the school of Baudelaire or of Valéry. He was right out of those swamps. We have to realize that, pay attention to that, and be faithful to it. Our tradition has always been a more populous and popular one. I think that this, too, is involved, but essentially there are a lot of writers out here now. Each issue of *American Review,* which is known for having high standards, publishes five, six, seven writers that we've never heard of before—really never heard of them. Right over that transom, as they call it, these writers come out of the blue. They don't always come from such places as Greenwich Village and Chicago. They are more likely to come from Salt Lake City; or High Point, North Carolina; or Wichita; San Jose—places that you wouldn't expect the important writers of our time to be coming from, but there they are. They're good; they're very good, very accomplished, crafted, well trained, and totally unknown, and they're legion.

So, I think it's not quite as simple as Mr. Boyers is saying. And for *American Poetry Review,* I would suppose its waywardness or its uneven standards—I call a certain kind of necessary eclecticism today—are such because there are so many different kinds of poetry being written. And who is to say that what looks to you like doggerel or words being flung down won't also turn out to be this generation's "Howl" or "Khaddish?"

I think what Stephen Berg is trying to do is to keep the doors open as wide as possible to create a certain welcoming effect to new talent. *Poetry* magazine was somewhat like a newsletter being circulated among three hundred of the "blessed," and I think that its impact on poetry was, in a sense, quite limited, and it also fostered a king of elitism, which in the fifties was slowly strangling American poetry. All those academic poets who were writing beautiful odes to their wives' toothbrushes and so on didn't really have any kind of necessary reason for being a poem other than to show how close you could come to Wallace Stevens or one of the other masters. *American Poetry Review* does have this—I call it a sort of blue-jeans openness—and some of the poetry is pretty sloppy, but, nonetheless, it is trying to span the range of poetry today which is very broad, very diverse, and so on.

I think that what we really need are more *Big Tables,* and, if it takes the National Endowment for the Arts to begin putting more money into it, then thank God that the National Endowment for the Arts has the money to do so, and so maybe it will reach a couple of thousand readers rather than a couple of hundred. Moreover, literary magazines were formerly being published a lot by publishing houses, so there was *Harper's*, which originally was *Harper's Press, Scribner's, Dial*—in more recent times *Evergreen Review*—and these magazines would have the muscle and re- sources and distribution and so on of the publishing houses be- hind them which would give them that much more influence and impact—status. Those don't exist anymore. There is only one that's being done, and that's *American Review*, and it's now in its third publishing house, and it has hardly been a smashing success as far as its stability goes. It is also down to two issues a year. And this is characteristic, I think, of the relation of publishing to literature. There's a long rap by me in the current issue about this parlous state of literary publishing today, which is more and more being abandoned by the New York houses who are cutting their lists of poetry and fiction and so on by 30, 40, 50 percent. You know, something has to begin to take up that slack, particularly with all these writers that I was talking about before. The little magazines with their adjacent small presses and the way that they have been getting into doing books as well as issues of their magazines are maybe the alternatives to what's happening in this contracting of the publishing market through the withdrawal of interest of publishing houses, or at least the modification of their interest. So there, too, an important area is involved with the little magazine developing books and publishing them and distributing them— books that the "hardcover houses" are turning their backs on these days.

Well, I guess since I have rambled on for a long time now, I'll shut up and turn over to you.

Alan Austin:

I am Alan Austin, editorial director of *Black Box*. Our time is very short and I'll try to be as brief as possible. I do want to talk a little about what we're doing. I also wanted to make one much shorter and simpler response to my friend Bob Boyers, who stunned me with his comment about Broadside Press poetry, as if that were a definable genre by anything other than the format of the books and the color of the writers.

It seems to me that questions of taste and rationality can too easily, if they're defined, have racist consequences. Now, I learned this the hard way, and that's why I work with a black coeditor. To say that—well, let that go.

This is *Black Box*. It has a pair of cassettes inside. Although people are usually very interested in it, I am going to skip all the mechanical things about how we do it to save time. Let me pick up somewhere in here. Rather obviously we have a bias in favor of work which moves beyond the conventions of written poetry. We are interested in work which takes the largest possible risk, whether in terms of psychic exposure by the poet, in terms of social statement, or in terms of performance technique. When we find a rare piece that manages to do all three of those things in one work, it goes into the next issue.

That's more mechanics, more mechanics. Now, why are we doing it? How did it come about? I think that it is worth doing. In the late sixties, I got a few random impressions of the literary scene in which I'd been working for ten years that began to puzzle me, and I didn't quite know what to do with them. The first was a fluke. From 1962 to 1969 I was literary editor of a magazine called *Motive*. *Motive* was a middle-sized, professionally-staffed monthly—political commentary, cultural analysis, the arts—and I was responsible for the poetry, the fiction, and the back of the book, the reviews. Because of a conflict—which we certainly won't go into—between the staff and the publisher, we had a couple of professional readership studies done. It was partly to establish what our real audience was. We found that with a paid circulation of 46,000 we had an actual audited readership of 135,000. More interestingly, we found that the only thing in the magazine which absolutely every reader read was the poetry. This was unheard of. I was very pleased, but I didn't know what to make of it; so I filed it away in the back of my head, in my personal pride file, and continued to brood on it.

The same thing I observed was that the audience for poetry readings had grown enormously in the late sixties and had undoubtedly come to exceed the audience for written poetry by a factor of ten or twenty or even one hundred. That came to me in an epiphany. I was in Iowa City. Robert Creeley was reading and had been booked into a hall that was much too small, so they had to move the reading to a very much larger auditorium. And I found myself *running*, with at least a thousand people, down a street in Iowa City to hear a poet read. And I looked around and I said, "My God, this is not the way I've been editing poetry. Something is going on here that's been unexamined."

The third observation came out of my own period of intense political activity in the late sixties—we can do without the details of that, too. I came away from a three-year period of deep political involvement. I came back to my writing and to literary editing with a very depressing sense of the innocence of most of the poets

and writers whom I knew and some anger, even, at the facility
with which poets had been able to take those phenomena which
we call racism, and imperialism, and sexism, and all those unpoet-
ic words, and make them material for their work without coming
to terms with the way those things affected the way they lived,
the way they published their work, and the categories into which
their work was divided and subdivided. To put it bluntly, it
seemed to me that at that time the literary scene was less progres-
sive and far less self-critical than the churches. And that's about
the most damning thing I can think of to say.

Now, I carried those observations around in my head. I was
also studying—by dumb luck, at the Institute for Policy Studies—
new developments in the mass media, and I was beginning to
write poetry again for the first time in several years. I came up
with four hypotheses that I wanted to test. First was a literary
hypothesis that the major new development, cutting across all
lines of race, class, sex, or educational background, was an intense
concern among poets for their own *real* voice and, as a conse-
quence, for their relationship to their audience. Second was a social hypothesis, and that was that the audience for poetry was now
much more interested in readings, much more interested in hearing poetry than in reading it in print. Third was a technological
hypothesis—which was solved very easily by getting some cost estimates—that audio-tape technology was a mature technology, generally available throughout the society, that it was growing more
popular, and it was also growing less expensive year by year, so
that it seemed a feasible way to do a magazine. Fourth was an
economic hypothesis that if new technology was adopted first and
on a nonprofit basis by poets and by friends of poets, it might
become a possible source of income for poets as well as a way of
reaching very much larger audiences.

Now those are the hypotheses. We have been testing them
through six issues, for three years, and it's time to make a report.
That's what I want to do. I have some good news and some bad
news. First the good news. The literary and social hypotheses are,
I think, unarguably true; they've been true beyond our wildest
expectations. We have about 500 paid subscribers for *Black Box*,
and, based on informal surveys, each of them shares their tapes
around with at least nine friends. That means an audience of at
least minimally 50,000 people for the tapes directly. Furthermore,
we've succeeded in making agreements with over forty radio sta-
tions to broadcast the tapes, provided we have time to re-edit
them into half-hour radio programs. Assuming a conservative average of 2,000 listeners on each station, which is very conservative, that is another 80,000 listeners. That means our minimum total audience, at this point, is 130,000 people. And it

doesn't count sales of back issues, which also continue to sell very well.

Now, the technological hypothesis is partly correct. The cost of tape equipment has decreased, and the production cost per copy has gone down spectacularly—it has gone down nearly 40 percent since our first issue. But it takes far more editorial time and expense and overhead than we ever thought it would. So I think our original estimates remain correct; the figures have shifted to different lines.

Now the bad news. Even with that large audience, we haven't found any acceptable mechanism to lift money from anyone but the five hundred people who buy the tapes, and, to put it bluntly, if we don't find a new source of subsidy or a new formula for devising our budget or a commercial distributor, we're going to be bankrupt by next June. We've got a rather lively tiger by the tail and we need help, if anyone has any ideas.

Now, what's to be learned by what we've done? We heard a lot yesterday about the life of the imagination and how that life is so ill served in America in the present economic and cultural conditions. The real question which has emerged from this conference, I think, and the question which we've sought to answer with *Black Box* is, Why is the life of the imagination served so imaginatively by editors and by publishers? We surely all know by now that audiences are made not born, and that you have to spend money and time and skill putting audiences together. Why don't we develop them? Why don't we discuss the strange phenomena of poets who are actually afraid of having audiences? Why don't we understand the trap we're all caught in and which came up yesterday at the small-press panel, where we substitute sales figures for real discussions of who our audiences are and how we relate to them? And, well, there's more. But these are the kinds of questions, I think, that form the literary agenda as a practical matter for the next ten to twelve years. And I'll leave it there.

Griffith:

Thank you. The panel this morning, I think, has been an interesting and varied panel in that those of you who are not in the publication of literary magazines or little magazines that are in our audience today have been treated to the full spectrum of what is available in terms of the format of such publications. My own *Poetry NOW* is a tabloid, newspaper-type publication, as is *American Poetry Review*. David Young's *Field* magazine is a square-back, primarily poetry and criticism magazine. Robert Boyers's *Salmagundi* is interested in the humanities as well as, in a broader sense, in simply the publication of poetry and fiction. Larry McMurtry is a novelist but has given us, I think, some very interesting perceptions and comments on the publication of short fiction, and the basic lack of a place to publish much short fiction, and the difficulties of a person who is primarily a novelist attempting to do short fiction in our country today. Ramona Weeks, with her *Inscape* and her Baleen Press is an instance of something I commented on, the little magazine that comes and goes. *Inscape,* as she has indicated, was a magazine that was birthed, lived a short time, died, and then after a period of years was resurrected, this time with an adjunct, a small press. Ted Solotaroff, of course, has his well-known *American Review,* certainly one of the best outlets of mass commercial distribution of poetry and fiction in the country today but not a magazine in the sense that most of us regard a magazine. It is really a mass-produced paperback book, which is a slightly different genre. And Alan Austin's *Black Box* is, again, a highly innovative type of publication, if you can call it a publication, in that it is, as he's indicated, two cassette tapes, and you get an audio magazine, you get poets reading. It has thus far been exclusively a poetry magazine, in that they have recorded no fiction.

Some of us, the members of this panel, were discussing at breakfast this morning how we related to the publication of fiction in particular, since we primarily are dealing with the publication of poetry. Ted Solotaroff and Larry McMurtry were not present, so it was the rest of us who were discussing this. But I'm glad that they have been able to bring some perceptions and observations to the publishing of fiction.

We would be glad to try to answer any questions or to hear any comments from the audience and have some dialogue with the audience, if anyone cares to speak. Clayton Eshleman.

Eshleman:

I'd like to address a question to all of the panel members who are presently editing or publishing a magazine. Is your magazine capable of existing on the basis of subscriptions and sales alone, and do you pay your contributors?

Griffith:

The question for the panel is—those who publish magazines, and this would apply also to the question of the tapes, as it were: Could your magazine exist solely on subscription alone?

Weeks:

Mine couldn't, no, and no, we don't pay contributors. And that's our next priority.

Griffith:

Okay.

Austin:

We could exist on subscription if we had fifteen hundred subscribers, and we're trying hard to get them. Because of the state
of the economy, we're not getting them, and we can't get them at
an acceptable cost this year. We do pay our contributors and the
current rate of payment is three dollars a minute, which sounds
enormous and isn't.

Solotaroff:

It's hard to say, because *American Review* is so locked in to a
whole publishing operation that produces sixty books a month.
Our covers, for example, are printed with nineteen other covers,
and that's why they only cost about two cents apiece. What it
would be like to publish 288 pages of writing, which is what's in
every issue, at $2.45 without the economies of the mass market,
no, I couldn't do it; it would be impossible. So I'm subsidized, in
effect, by Bantam Books.

Griffith:

Okay. Larry, unless you have some comment, we'll go to Bob.

Boyers:

Well, at this point, *Salmagundi* could exist without a subsidy,
but it would exist in a different way. That is to say, we'd have
somewhat fewer pages, we'd have a somewhat different range of
contributors, and clearly we'd reach a very different and more
limited audience. For example, lots of the people that we reach,
we reach through advertising in the *New York Review of Books*
and places of that kind, and if we didn't have the subsidy, we
couldn't advertise. As for paying contributors, we do pay contributors for special issues which are turned into paperback or hardbound books and which further support the magazine. Contributors to those issues do get paid, but contributors to general issues,
which are not turned into books, don't get paid.

Young:

I think that we have about six hundred subscribers, and we sell
about three hundred to four hundred copies of the magazine. If
we could double that, we would be self-supporting. We pay contrib-

utors, and that is fluctuated a little bit because we have once or twice had grants, and then we have been able to increase our rate of payment. But the standard for a long time was ten dollars a page; now it is up to fifteen dollars, and, while a grant lasted, it was at twenty dollars.

Griffith:

I'll reply also for *Poetry NOW*. We are not able to pay our subscribers—our contributors, rather—at this point in time. Within another year we expect to be able to operate on subscriptions. We have been very lucky in that we have been taken up by a number of writing courses in universities as a supplemental text. And with an expense from this and with a general growth of subscriptions, we think that this will be able to stabilize the magazine from its own resources, but . . . Peter?

Davison:

I'd like to ask Alan Austin a question. To expatiate more on what you said about the problem of poets who don't want an audience, I'd love to hear a little more from you on that.

Austin:

Well, it's something I've just begun to discover, and it comes up in phrases that people use in declining to get involved in what we're doing. The most recent one, the one that's sticking on my mind at the moment, is one where we're in the process of doing a somewhat megalomaniacal project of trying to record every working poet in the Washington, D.C., area, for which we got a special grant and from which we'll do a lot of things. But I mentioned that we've so far recorded over two hundred people, and one poet said to me, "I wouldn't want to get involved in anything that large." Very strange, very strange. The more common form it takes, the first form in which I noticed it, is a severe mike fright that many poets experience—perhaps half the poets whom we work with, which is actually a small percentage of the tape we get, most of the tape comes in already done. How frightened of their voices, how frightened of being heard the poets are. We've all seen this in novices at public readings. Somehow the thought of actually sending a poem out at large to unknown faceless people, embodied only in the voice, is very frightening, which has surprised me.

Davison:

Fear of the audience or fear of technology?

Austin:

I think it's fear of the audience.

Griffith:

Two interesting viewpoints. I think there is something very interesting that Alan touched on in his comments about the editing of the tapes that they are doing for *Black Box* for ultimate broadcast, in that there you do reach a different and much broader audience through technology than you might reach through either the purchase of the individual cassettes or even through the publication of some of our magazines. Other questions? Yes?

Dana Hay:

I'm Dana Hay. Although we might wish to throw at Mr. Boyers terms of endearment, we would suggest, along with Reed Whittemore, that there is room in our culture for political poetry. Also, I would further wish to suggest to Mr. Boyers that before he continues to make his comments about black English and black poetry, he would perhaps wish to be aware that there are linguists in England as well as on this side of the Atlantic who believe that black English is a *true* language, worthy to be read and worthy to be written. We would also suggest to Mr. Boyers that he might wish to read more black poetry, he might wish to talk with people who speak black English, and, in so doing, he might even find—as I truly believe that he would—that black poetry would truly reach even his soul.

Griffith:

We have time for a few more questions.

Boyers:

I would prefer to respond to that.

Griffith:

Bob, would you care to comment, please.

Boyers:

Yes. Well, first of all, of course, I did not address myself to black poetry, a phenomenon of black English which is a subject entirely, it seems to me, outside the range of our present discussion. I did refer, purely as an illustrative case in point, to the Broadside Press, which seems to me to have cultivated an audience which is not essentially interested in poetry as an art form, but which is interested in poetry and other statements as political incentive and political action-theater, which, by the way I should mention, seems to me perfectly legitimate. I'd make no suggestions that the sources of publication be closed to anyone who wishes to write or to publish. Everyone has, obviously, a perfect right to express himself or herself as he wishes. The issue really has nothing to do with whether or not black poets, or Chicano poets, or poor white poets, or any poet has a right to express himself. The issue, as I was trying to raise it, has to do with the high culture, as it were, and I'm unashamedly interested in poetry as a manifestation of the high culture. And I'm interested in poetry as art, which has, it seems to me, to make certain kinds of discriminations which editors and writers themselves will regularly have to make as they go about their business. To bring in, by way of further response, something that Mr. Solotaroff said, to the effect that who was to say that what looks to you or to me like doggerel today won't turn out to be the next generation's "Howl" or "Khaddish" seems to me finally not to engage the fact that as an editor and as a reader one has to make discriminations. That is to say, if something which is submitted to me as an editor or as a reader seems to be doggerel, I'll have to respond to it as doggerel, and I'll have to reject it on that basis. If the next generation makes it into a holy book, well that's fine. You know, I'm willing to accept the fact that I may not see what the next generation will do.

One further word. I might mention that to refer to the stuff in *Big Table* as though it had been routinely censored over a long period of time by the high literary culture of this country is to, it seems to me, foster a mistaken impression. I grew up in the fifties, and *Naked Lunch,* and "Howl," and *The Subterraneans,* and so on were books that were given to me when I was in college in the fifties. It didn't take these people very long at all to meet a mass audience or a highly literate audience in the universities. So I don't think that the fact of the matter is that these particular people, the best poets and writers and so on, were censored in any serious way in this country, just to speak from my own experience of them.

Griffith:

Further comments? Questions? Yes?

Audience:

This conference has been concentrating much more on poetry than on fiction. I'd like to ask a question of Mr. McMurtry. Could,

perhaps, the marketing and publishing in periodicals of serious
fiction be more successful if you returned to a marketing technique that worked for the best-selling nineteenth-century novelists
like Charles Dickens, and worked in the early period of this century, and works now for the science-fiction writers, namely, the
combination of serialization of a novel in the same issue of a magazine that publishes shorter fiction also, instead of the practice of
excerpting?

McMurtry:

My own opinion would be no. I don't think it would work now,
I just don't believe that the mechanism is there. I'm not even sure
that the appetite is there, frankly. Had I not been hurrying, I
would have complimented Mr. Solotaroff when I spoke first, because I think he is practically the only editor of anything resembling a magazine that I can think of that offers some outlet to
quality short fiction. He's really the only alternative to the *New
Yorker,* so far as I am concerned. But from the point of view of
the young and developing writer, the really disastrous thing is
something that Mr. Solotaroff also mentioned, which is that hardback book publishers just aren't publishing much fiction anymore.
They're publishing only about a third as many first novels in a
given year as they were publishing twelve, fifteen years ago. I
have seen and passed on several manuscripts—first novels—that I
thought were superior to my own first novel, that have gone
around New York and Boston for five and six and seven years,
and sometimes not been published at all, although they certainly
would have been published in the late fifties or even up as far as
the mid- or late sixties. And I think that young writers are flexible
and resilient enough that they can do without a particular form.
I doubt that there are so many people, so many writers who are
intrinsically short-story writers and only short-story writers, that
they can't adjust to the difficulties of publishing short fiction, and
write long fiction, or write something else. But if they can't publish either short fiction or long fiction and get any satisfactory
response to it, then they are in trouble. And they are in trouble
right now. I just don't see, myself, any real possibility for a return
to serial fiction.

Solotaroff:

I would have to agree. Moreover, I would say that, given the
appalling dearth of outlets of any influence for shorter fiction, to
take those few pages there are—such as in *American Review*—and
use them to run chapters of a novel which is then going to be

published anyway in its own suitable form—which is the book it-self—would, I think, be wrong. My feeling is that what may well have to happen is a similar development in fiction to what is oc-curring in poetry, that if you look around you, you find that in poetry, which has been the most neglected area of commercial publishing, poets have taken matters more into their own hands. And they're much more involved now, not just in writing poetry, but in printing it and in distributing it, in arranging audiences for it, or bringing it into the schools, bringing it into sort of a public forum. That old system of waiting for Houghton Mifflin to call and say, "Yes we'll take your book and make you famous, if not rich," is being replaced by an awareness that maybe we have to begin to do our own kinds of publishing and create our own dis-tribution and so on. I think this is a very important development, and it wouldn't surprise me if I look around and see things like the Fiction Collective that's sprung up—and I'm sure there will be others—to see more fiction being published this way. I mean, New York publishing is very limited. People there keep both ears to the ground, so they don't really see very far. And so you can't just depend on New York to do the job, and I think you have to begin to look elsewhere for fiction as well as poetry.

Griffith:

I think one thing, too, that it's easy to blame television as the monster that is responsible for all sorts of things and changes in our society, but I think that the advent of television as an enter-tainment form is something that has definitely helped to spell the death—or the illness, if not death—of the short story as a form. When I was in my teens and early twenties growing up, I read short stories, as many of my generation did, as a form of enter-tainment. Television now, in canned form, one hour long, one-half hour long per episode, brings you an equivalent story. You can't say that television in any way is comparable to, say, the fic-tion of Hemingway, Faulkner, Katherine Anne Porter—the peo-ple whose short stories I've read and admired in my growing years. But, it ends up a contemporary equivalent as an entertain-ment form. You do get a story in any TV episode; it has a plot, it has character, it has the advantage for people who do not have vivid imaginations to vivify the characters they read about, in that it's all being acted out before you, in color. So, that is a benefactor also.

McMurtry:

Could I speak on that just a second? I would just like to say that as a fiction writer I feel no sense of competition or threat from any other media. I don't feel that I am in competition with television, with movies, with rock music. But I do feel that I'm in competition with journalism, and I think that if there has been a declining market for serious and interesting fiction, the real competitors are the new journalists, many of whom are very good, very astute. They tell stories, too. They have appropriated to themselves many of the techniques of fiction while retaining the appeal of fact, and I think that is where the readership of fiction has gone.

Griffith:

That's an excellent point. Yes?

Audience:

Are the decisions that you have to make on fiction as tough as those you have to make on poetry? That is, I can sympathize with those people who say, "Let's talk more about fiction," but as an editor I don't have the backlog of good fiction that I have of good poetry. I don't think that there are as many people writing good fiction as there are writing good poetry.

Solotaroff:

I'm sorry, was that to me? Oh. We get now, about 8,000 fiction manuscripts a year, which is roughly about 200 a week. And about 50 of those come from agents, and about 150 come over the transom; and 80 percent of the fiction that we get, you know, has sort of been intercepted on its way to *Good Housekeeping* or other journals that also appear in *Writer's Digest.* The 20 percent that's left is stuff that everyone reads and that we deliberate about carefully, and I would say I could publish four times as much fiction as I do. Now, at two issues a year, I publish about twenty stories a year, or works of prose, or fiction. And I could publish at least a hundred without reducing the quality of what I'm doing. And so, I find it desperately difficult to make these choices. I feel sort of like choosing between children oftentimes. And I really do. It just breaks the heart to send back three-fourths of the stories that I have to send back among that group that I consider, because they're eminently publishable. And it just makes me sore, finally. I mean after all the politeness and all the abstractions and generalizations and so on, that this society with its resources and wealth and so on has such a piss-poor literary publishing apparatus. . . .

Griffith:

All right, we will allow three more questions. We're running beyond our time. This is very interesting, but there is another panel to follow, and there's the matter of lunch in between. So, first of the three. Make them relatively short, if you can.

Audience:

Well, quickly, I am curious as to what you say to these authors in that three-fourths group that you reject. Do they get the same old stuff that the others, who you don't feel so badly about, get? I would classify your expression of sorrow and I wondered if you—

Solotaroff:

I'll answer your question very fast. I write letters. I send rejection slips to people that I have nothing to say to because their story or poem said nothing to me. That 20 percent, I would say virtually all of them get letters that say, look, you know, this is swell. I finally am not going to publish it because the ending doesn't quite leave the mark I thought it would, or it's a ways getting into. But finally, I'm publishing a fraction, a pitiful fraction of the material I should be publishing, and, alas, I can't publish this one. But I also try to let that letter reflect what made the story stand in my mind and what made me consider it as carefully as I did. I mean, that's the least I can do, along with what is finally a rejection.

Griffith:

Okay. Two more questions, if there are two. Yes?

Audience:

What about your reading as an outlet for short fiction? I can go to a poetry reading almost once a week in Washington. It seems to me that if the short fiction is good, it will be received, it will draw a lot of people and draw a lot of attention to fiction. The poets have been doing that successfully for at least a decade.

Griffith:

All right, the question, in case anyone did not hear it, basically is: Why is not the reading of fiction, particularly the short story, an alternative mode of circulation, as it were, in the same way that the reading of poetry is? Any comments?

McMurtry:

I don't know, frankly. There's no tradition for it, that's all I can say. I've never been invited to read.

Griffith:

Ted, any comment from you?

Solotaroff:

I just think it's a swell idea, and I think that one of the ways in which fiction writers can begin to organize themselves in the way that the poets have is to have a kind of fiction-reading circuit in much the same as has developed this reading circuit, and lots of things have come out of that, including, you know, finally a much larger public awareness of poetry.

Griffith:

Okay, our final question.

Boyers:

Can I address myself to this for a moment? There is a small handful of prose writers, fiction writers, who do go around and read. Several of them have come to my school, Skidmore, but I think that one of the problems with disseminating prose fiction that way, especially short prose fiction, is that American fiction writers themselves have been ambivalent, at best, about the status of the short story. Many of the best fiction writers in the United States, for example, have used the writing of short fiction as a stepping stone to do larger and, by their lights, much more important things. Many of them, for example, have come to give up writing the short story entirely, seeing it as a kind of training ground in which you refine your craft and then go on to do the thing that's really important, which is writing novels. You can think for yourselves of the full range of American fiction writers who started out with a slender volume of very good short stories, and who then went on to write novels, many of them very unsuccessful. I can think, just off the top of my head, of people like Irvin Faust, who ten years ago published a magnificent book of stories called *Roar Lion Roar,* and then went on to write four or five not-very-good novels, feeling that that's the way you make it as a fiction writer in America, or that's the way you fail. Or think of someone like Hortense Calisher, a magnificent short-story writer who turned to writing thoroughly, by my lights, unsuccessful novels. And you could go on and on and name many others. And that may be one of the reasons why there really is not much of a market for people to come around and read short stories. It's not the thing.

Griffith:

One final question. John.

John C. Broderick:

I'd just like to add a footnote on this question. We have had short-story writers read at the Library of Congress—John Updike, Peter Taylor, John Barth, and a good many others. Last season we had Joyce Carol Oates, and our original intention was that she would read some of her fiction and her poetry. She was much more willing to read her poetry than she was her fiction, and Mr. McMurtry will be getting a letter from us soon.

Griffith:

Final question.

Audience:

I would like to address a question to Mr. Solotaroff or Mr. McMurtry. As a foreigner in this country, I see that the short story in Latin America and Europe is so popular to all classes, to all people, and not here. What has happened to the short story? Do you have any explanation why it is not popular in America and it is popular in Russia and Europe and Latin America?

Griffith:

The question is, Why, in the opinion of Mr. Solotaroff and Mr. McMurtry, is the short story not popular in the United States in the same way that it is in Latin America, Europe, and other places? Ted?

Solotaroff:

Well, you know, there is certainly the drying up of the market that's come from the decline of magazines that were publishing short fiction. Even the *Saturday Evening Post* would occasionally publish a story by William Faulkner or a lesser name and enable that writer to live for a year on what that story earned. So there was a kind of motive, an economic motive for writing stories, which is less and less the case, because there are just fewer magazines that are publishing fiction, and those that are publishing it tend to publish less of it than they did in the past. I think that Mr. McMurtry has put his finger on something quite important, which is the way in which new journalism, or journalism in general, has tended to deflect interest. Short stories, like novels, brought the news, too, except they brought the news of the inner life of the society: what was going on behind the scenes that the newspapers reported on. People read fiction as a way of staying in touch with that inner life. A lot of that now, you know, is being touched upon by writers like Tom Wolfe and so on, and it comes in more palatable form. It's faster, it's breezier, it's brisker, and so on. I mean every issue of *New York* magazine probably has the seed of eight stories or novels in it, and the material is being used up in the *New York* way of packaging it—sort of like bacon. As a result, though, I think that writers who would be encouraged to write stories or who would write stories have been discouraged, because how do they market them? I think it's as simple as that, isn't it, Larry?

McMurtry:

Yes, I really think so. I think fiction writers tend to write what they can get paid for, and if they can't get paid for it they pretty soon stop writing it. I think there is one other thing I might say, which is, I suspect in the countries you mention there is still more leisure than there is in America, and because there's more leisure there is really more tolerance for minor writing. I think what the new journalism or journalism has done in America is simply to cut the gound out from under second- and third-rate fiction, which was, after all, the great reading staple throughout the nineteenth and well into the twentieth century. The novel of information, the short story of what it's like to grow up in Maine in a fishing village, or something like that, we don't need anymore, because we get that information from documentary journalism of various kinds. There is no patience left in America for the minor fiction writer. The pressure to be better, the pressure to be absolutely first-rate gets more intense all the time.

Solotaroff:

There's Dick Seaver up there. Do you still want to ask it?

Griffith:

We'll permit one final question. Dick Seaver.

Seaver:

My comment is directed to Mr. Boyers. For your information, I was the editor on *Naked Lunch,* the book publication, and I just want to disabuse his idea that there was a very short period of time between the Chicago suppression or problems that arose there and the book publication. It cost about $50,000 and fifteen years to settle the court cases, and I submit that it took the efforts of a publisher to bring that accessibility. It was not that easy, and I think there are books, especially if they are different, that will present problems that have to be cooperated with.

Griffith:

We're going to have to conclude our panel. I want to thank our panelists for participating and all of you who are attending. We hope you'll attend the 2:30 panel on the survival of the writer, which will be chaired by Len Randolph. Thank you.

Survival of the Writer: Support by Organizations and Foundations

Leonard Randolph, chairman; Donald Barthelme; Kathleen Fraser; Elizabeth Kray; Barbara Ringer; Grace Schulman; Galen Williams

Kunitz:

We have arrived at the final session of our conference. I began the proceedings yesterday morning. It seems much longer than that since we started, but I began the proceedings by saying that the publishing industry is in a state of crisis and that what I believed we were going to discuss was not so much the economics of publishing as the survival of the life of the imagination in this country. Nothing has been said during the course of our proceedings that has made me qualify that judgment. I think we are discussing terribly serious matters.

One of the conclusions—I've learned a lot, incidentally, from this conference. There's so many ideas floating through my head that it will take me some time before I can crystallize what I feel has to be done to rectify the situation insofar as it concerns writing or the plight of writers in this country. One thing seems to be very clear, and I hope I'm not distorting the picture when I say that the first observable fact is that trade publishing is no longer adequate or, perhaps, is no longer willing to meet its responsibilities in relation to serious writing.

Another phenomenon which I think has emerged clearly is that the hope for the future seems to lie out in the sticks, out throughout the rest of this country, where the small presses and the little magazines are struggling for survival—struggling desperately because they have no means, really, to permit them to continue unless they get some help. Where are they going to get that help? I suppose the answer must be either they get it through

119

some sort of affiliation with the publishing industry, with the now mainly conglomerate enterprises that control American publishing, or else through institutional and organizational support of some kind, through some sort of public funding, perhaps.

The members of this panel come largely out of that world, and I think that we must turn to them with some hope that they can provide us with some of the answers we are looking for. The chairman of the panel is Leonard Randolph, who is the director of the Literature Program for the National Endowment for the Arts and has been that since 1966. He's himself a poet and understands these problems, understands them very well. I know, because he was the first person I turned to when the idea for this conference arrived, and he has been enormously helpful, not only in securing financial support but in advising us on the conduct of the whole program.

Before the panel starts, I've been asked, for a small interruption, to introduce Ahmos Zu-Bolton for a rather grave announcement. Will you please be brief?

Ahmos Zu-Bolton:

This morning I drove up to the hotel where some of the panelists were staying to pick up Dudley Randall, Broadside Press, and there was a note. The note said that Mr. Randall had had a mild heart attack and he was at Rogers Memorial Hospital. I went to see him, and he seems all right, in good spirits. He asked for a folder with some work of his, and I went back and got it. I called his wife, and she said that he had a history of such heart attacks, and he would be in the hospital there for a couple of days. When I got over here, I found out that there was a lot of discussion this morning concerning Broadside Press, concerning Mr. Randall's expertise as a publisher. It seems that black poets always get that, so we're kind of used to it. It seems ironic that Mr. Randall is still getting that, after all this time, after he published Audre Lorde, who was nominated for a National Book Award, which a lot of times, in the old days, we used to say was the white folks' award. She was nominated for a book coming out of his press for one of the so-called white folks' awards. He's still getting that, but that's cool, you know. I just want to say, a sort of editorial remark, that Brother Randall gave black poets a chance to publish when a lot of people wouldn't even look at our manuscripts, and we owe him a big debt. I don't know how anybody else feels about him, but I think that maybe some gesture from the Library would be appreciated. He's at Rogers Memorial Hospital, if anybody wants to go over and maybe see him or send him something. Thank you.

Leonard Randolph:

Thank you, Ahmos. So far as the tenor and the tone and the overall meaning and the impact of this conference are concerned, I think the majority of us in this audience, and certainly I know myself, and I believe the majority of the people on the stage right now would like to say that Dudley Randall has made a major contribution to American literature. He has found ways to put the work of a large number of very serious, very experimental, and eventually very worthwhile black writers in print. He has also found ways, I think, of distributing those works beyond the wildest imaginations of most people who are involved in small-press publishing; 140,000 copies of a work by Don Lee is not to be sneezed at by a damn sight, not only by the small presses but also by the commercial publishers in this country. You sat here yesterday morning, and you heard one representative after another of the trade publishers say that they could not sell more than 1,000 or 1,500 or 2,000 copies of a book of poetry. Okay? Alongside 140,000, that makes Dudley look pretty damn good, I think.

Aside from that, this is something I feel compelled to say. I had not intended to feel emotional about it, because I hadn't realized that Dudley had had a heart attack. I long ago became very impatient, weary, bone tired, as a matter of fact, of hearing academic people talk about high art and low art and talk about poetry as though it ought to be limited to an audience of five in the entire world. Whitman said, "To have great poets, you must have great audiences." Whitman was, I think, a very wise man. He also freed up poetry a great deal, and he's read a hell of a lot more, nowadays, by more people than a lot of those people who would like to count the readers of poetry on the fingers of one hand.

Stanley, I should clear up one thing before Carolyn Kizer descends on us. I have not been the director of the Literature Program since 1966; I've been with the endowment since 1966, going through a wide variety of jobs, including sweeping the floor and doing press releases and cutting stencils and everything else, back in the days when we had a staff of twenty. I have been director of the Literature Program since 1970, when Carolyn Kizer left. Carolyn was the first director of the program, and a splendid director she was. She did an awful lot with a very, very small amount of money, and, for myself, I love her dearly. I admire the work she has done, especially the work she's doing most recently, and I feel privileged and honored to follow in her footsteps in this job.

I'd like to introduce the members of the panel for this afternoon, and I should tell you that they have been warned under

penalty of death, all save one of them, that they must confine
their remarks to no more than five or six minutes, because we
want to leave plenty of time this afternoon for questions from the
audience. I know the members of the panel are far more interested in that than we are in making speeches at you, including myself. One exception to that rule, because of the enormous com-
plexity of the subject with which she has to deal, is Ms. Barbara
Ringer, who is the register of copyrights, and I think any of you
who know anything at all about the copyright laws in the United
States and know about the enormous struggle that has gone on
for all these years toward a revision of the copyright laws will
understand that Ms. Ringer does need some additional time to be
able to deal with that subject with any kind of honesty and clarity
at all. So she has told me that she needs about fifteen or twenty
minutes, and we're delighted to have her speak for that long, and
we hope that we'll be a lot more enlightened about copyright than
we were when she began.

The first member of the panel I would like to introduce is a
guy who really turned American prose on its ear and American
publishing on its ear, I think, a very, very splendid short-fiction
writer, Donald Barthelme. And to Donald's immediate left, the
former director of the Poetry-in-the-Schools program in the Bay
area and northern California, and director of the San Francisco
Poetry Center, a splendid poet herself, Kathleen Fraser. And the
executive director of the Academy of American Poets, which is
America's single most dedicated and devoted organization dealing
with the everyday lives of poets and with trying to bring recognition to them, both in their early, their middle, and their declining
years, Elizabeth Kray—Betty Kray. And now, immediately to Betty's left is Ms. Barbara Ringer, the register of copyrights. Next,
Grace Schulman, director of the largest and the longest running
series of poetry readings in the country, YM-YWHA Poetry Center in New York. And last but by no means least—and you'll know
what I mean when I tell you that I think that Galen Williams and
I have gone through more bad times together and good times
together since I became director of the Literature Program than
almost anyone else in the country, because she has suffered with
me through the birth pangs and the eventual birth of the *Directory
of American Poets* and the forthcoming *Directory of American
Fiction Writers*—Galen Williams, the executive director of Poets &
Writers, Incorporated, in New York.

I have a prepared statement, which I normally do not have. If I
seem to stumble and clutter up the atmosphere with falling pages,
you'll know it's because I'm not accustomed to speaking from text.
I'm going to depart from it anyway, very briefly, about halfway
through.

It is logical that a conference devoted to the publication of poetry and fiction should end with a panel on the survival of writers. Even if we could solve all the problems of publication, the future of fiction and poetry in contemporary society ultimately lies with the individual writer and the individuals who buy and read his or her work.

Ideally the writer's support—all of it—would come from payment for the writer's creative output, whether that payment came from a trade publisher or a small press, a commercial magazine or a literary quarterly. With few exceptions, that has never been true in our society. For every man or woman who has "made a living" through serious creative writing, there have traditionally been a hundred or more who did not. Serious writers have been bricklayers, dishwashers, house painters, male nurses, secretaries, assistant professors, truck drivers, and insurance company executives. They have created work for themselves in nearly every wage-earning capacity we could identify in every decade of our two centuries. They are still doing it today and very likely will continue to do so in the future.

In some respects that may not be as undesirable and destructive as it seems, superficially. There is, after all, a certain enrichment, a cross-fertilization, to be gained from two simultaneous and serious vocations. William Carlos Williams comes immediately to mind. But in most regards, a good creative writer can function best and most productively when he or she has sufficient time—physically and mentally—to devote to the serious pursuit of craft. A block of time, even a few weeks or months free of the pressures of other responsibilities, may mean the difference between a truly finished novel or collection of poems and the frustrations of unfinished or half-realized work.

For this reason, outright fellowships are among the most valuable means of assisting good writers. The fellowships provided by private, philanthropic organizations and, more recently, by the Arts Endowment, represent support at a modest but meaningful level for a limited number of writers each year.

Despite the fact that the number of such fellowships has increased during the past few years, it is obvious that there will not be enough money, right away, to reach all writers whose work and careers deserve support. Last year, for example, the Literature Program received 1,600 applications in the fellowship program for creative writers. We were able to fund $5,000 fellowships for 155 of them. This time around, we have been able to raise the amount of each fellowship to $6,000 and will have enough money to award 165, thanks in large part to a transfer of $60,000 from the theater program, funds by the theater panel to specifically award 10 additional playwrights grants during the coming year. But the number of applications this time jumped to 2,400—800 more than we got last time. That means that we must counterbalance those 165 satisfied recipients against 2,235 less-than-happy and frustrated constituents in the field. This is not to say that all of those 2,235 should be said, automatically, to deserve fellowship support. There are a number whose work is at the very earliest stages of development, others whose interest in writing is primarily avocational, and still others who are engaged in writing and research more nearly allied to other areas. Yet, of the 1,400-plus applicants we were forced to reject in 1974, there were, in the opinion of the independent readers and Literature Program panelists, another 25 to 40 writers above the 155, whose work clearly would have justified recognition had sufficient funds been available.

The possibility that such money will miraculously appear is remote. We need, then, to think of "support" for writers in broader terms than just direct funding. Since we recognize the writer's need for gainful employment, for putting bread on the table, it is helpful to try to find ways of assuring jobs in areas related, in some way, to the poet or fiction writer's craft. Charles Olson once said, "If you want to really help a poet, give him another craft, that he can earn a living by." What we're trying to do now is to find other crafts that are related to the actual writing of poetry or the actual writing of fiction in which the writer can be engaged, which will not necessarily destroy not only his energy but also his desire to write.

The basic assumption underlying the endowment's program placing writers in elementary and secondary schools is just that. This year, after eight years of slow but steady growth, there will be an estimated one thousand poets and fiction writers in this program in each of the fifty states. The growth of the program, incidentally, has been slow and steady only because of funding limitations. One state arts council official told me last week that he could increase the number of projects in his state by at least 300 percent right now if he only had the money.

Although a program of this kind is valuable to writers because it does provide part-time—and in increasing numbers, full-time—employment, the benefits are actually more extensive and meaningful. Wherever I go, nationwide, writers who have worked in the program tell me that their day-to-day relationship with young people has had a powerful and beneficial impact on their own work.

It is just as important, I think, to look at the effect such a program has on the creative writer in his own community and state.

Eight years ago, none of the state and community arts agencies were reasonably cognizant of the number of serious writers in their area and had no sense of the needs of those writers when they came to their attention. Today, writers are not only serving on arts council staffs and being appointed to their governing boards but are beginning to receive fellowships and take an active part in the overall planning for the arts.

In earlier discussions, this conference has touched on the current problems of publishing in the trade, the small presses and university presses and in magazines. It is totally accurate to say that support for publication of any kind is also support for the individual writer. Without access to print, the writer's career cannot develop and flourish.

I think that one of the things that we have learned is that where the Literature Program is concerned, you have to crawl before you walk, because literature has never been recognized in this country by the private foundations, by municipal government, even by the education system as being one of the arts. When the Literature Program was first started, as a matter of fact, back in 1967, one of the questions that was asked was, Why isn't that program in the Humanities Endowment? Aside from the fact that writing a poem or writing a short story or a novel or a play is obviously an act of creativity and therefore an art, you cannot, sometimes, win that argument with people who insist upon believing that anything that is called literature has to be in a textbook and belongs in the humanities.

So the problem has been, for the past six or seven years, to convince people like the state arts councils that writers are artists, that they deserve support as artists, and that literature itself is one of our first and one of our most enduring art forms. What has happened because of the Poetry-in-the-Schools program is that the work the poets have been able to get out of the children and the work that has been created by the teachers—the volumes of poetry, the process of writing that has occurred particularly in the elementary schools—have brought about a remarkable change within communities. This year, for the first time, the endowment was able to fund two pilot projects placing poets or fiction writers within communities on a limited basis, to see what would happen. One of the projects was in Glendive, Montana, and the second is now going on in Olivia, Minnesota. They're both very small towns, and the effect that the writers have on the community, the effects were absolutely outstanding. In Glendive, Michael Moss, the poet who worked there, did an oral history with a lot of the older people in the community. He conducted workshop classes; every Monday night he had an adult class; he worked with the kids in the day camps, in the park nearby. And they all ended up with an

anthology of about sixty-five pages which contains a rather aston-
ishingly large number of works that could be worked on and
turned into very good poems. In Olivia, Minnesota, Joe Paddock
is not only doing workshops, he's doing the oral history. He's writing a column for the local weekly newspaper; he has met every
week with the service clubs in that area; he has talked with the
adult education groups; and, in general, he is going to end up, I
think, at the end of a nine-month residency there, with a body of
work which will represent a rather remarkable cross section of
that whole community.

All of those things happened with a very, very small amount of
money, first of all, and secondly, with one individual creative person being let loose in the community to bring out the creative
urges and the creativity of the people who already live there. We
hope that, eventually, this concept of placing poets and fiction
writers in the areas in which their presence will be most practical
and amenable will be able to spread not only to communities but
also to museums, to bookstores, to libraries, to any number of
other institutions within communities nationwide. One of the
things we are fascinated by right now, so far as support of writers
is concerned, is the CETA program, the Comprehensive Employment Training Act program, with which we've had a lot of luck in
some cities, particularly in San Francisco and Seattle, and in Min-
neapolis-St. Paul, in getting writers brought in to work on specific
projects as part of this modern-day version of the WPA.

All of those things we need to talk about this afternoon, we need
questions about them after the panelists have finished. I think
that, in conclusion, if this conference produces some signs for
direction for the future—and I think it has done that already—if
it holds up some trouble signs for us, tells us we're going in the
wrong direction sometimes, that's good too. If it does those things
and at the same time calls attention to the individual writer and
editor as an artist of equal standing in society with the good dan-
cer or actor or musician, then it will have served a purpose far
beyond its own time. We have to remember that one of the most
productive or profitable things that can come out of a conference
of this kind is not really the conference itself but the transcript
that comes after, because those things go on forever, and it's a
useful piece of information to mail people when they ask you
questions about particular things. There you have a body of expertise that you can just ship out to them in the mail.

Okay, thank you very much, and we'll turn to Donald.

Donald Barthelme:

Thank you, Leonard. I call your attention to the fact that the title of this panel is "The Survival of the Writer." I must tell you the first thing that I did when I arrived here this morning is borrow twenty-five bucks from John Broderick, our host, because I'd left home without bringing any money with me. But I had one of those little plastic cards, and luckily the airline allowed me to ride from New York to Washington.

I want to speak very briefly about an initiative that is now under way in the publishing line. You've heard from the commercial publishers, I judge, yesterday—although I wasn't here—sad stories of grim necessities which force them not to publish quality literary works. You heard, again this morning, of the necessity of writers taking things in their own hands. The project I'm going to tell you about speaks to both of these questions.

The main difficulty with the book business is that a book is two kinds of objects. You have, on one hand, a thing that a reasonable and prudent man might decide is a book. You have on the other hand an object which looks very much like a book, feels very much like a book, but is in actuality a bucket of peanut butter covered with a thin layer of chocolate sauce. These things are sold in the same way. The latter seems to sell better, for some mysterious reason, than the former. A good example of this that I ran into recently is a book called *The First Time,* which apparently has to do with accounts of initial sexual experiences of either eminent or reasonably well-known people. This, I would say, was a bucket of peanut butter. Actually, they missed. They should have done a book called *The Last Time,* which would not only be funnier but more poignant. That idea is copyrighted, by the way. Take notes.

What has happened is this. For a long time, a number of writers have been talking about setting up a writers' co-op on the model of the Swedish cooperative and the West German cooperative. In the case of the Swedish cooperative, the writers' co-op now sells as many or more books as the leading Swedish publishing house, Bonniers. The West German effort, which originally split off of the extremely good West German house of Suhrkamp, is doing equally well. We have gotten together a board of directors, which consists of a number of established writers and a lesser number of relatively unknown writers, and we are now coming forward to various funding groups, including the National Endowment, with proposals. The original directors include people like Renata Adler, Norman Mailer, Susan Sontag, myself, Jack Barth, Jack Hawkes, Walker Percy, Louise Glück, and some others—Ted Mooney, who is a young writer whose first publication was in Ted Solotaroff's *American Review,* in the current issue; Michelle Wallace, a young, black woman writer who's writing now for the *Village Voice*—about fourteen people in all. We filed articles of in-

corporation. We have worked out a carefully detailed program for
the publication of fifty books a year. The books would be in the
following categories: fiction, poetry, and so-called lost books.
There's a matter of scandal that, for example, most of the works
of the great English novelist Henry Green are not in print in this
country. The American examples are too numerous to list. The
lost books category is a Sargasso Sea filled with extremely valuable
work which is being kept from the public by the venality of the
commercial publishers. This effort, therefore, would be in those
three areas. It's also designed to get my younger brother's book
published. I have a younger brother whose name is Frederick
Barthelme, who's an extremely good writer. He's published one
collection of short stories with Winter House and a novel with
Doubleday, and he's having great difficulty getting his new book
published. It may have something to do with the fact that he's my
brother. As a matter of fact, I'm just publishing a book called *The
Dead Father,* and when he heard the title, he called me and said
he was at work on a book called *The Dead Brother.* So a secret
motive behind all this effort, which is a lot of effort, is to get my
younger brother's book published.

But anyhow, the interesting point to me about this, besides the
care with which everybody has contributed to working out the
proposal, is the magnitude of the proposal. We are asking for in
excess of a million dollars for the first three years; $1,100,000 and
change is the scale of the proposal. And this is deliberate. It's our
feeling that literary groups, literary magazines, and, indeed, writers themselves have been content over many years to ask for
crumbs, really, from the various funding organizations. Whereas
the performing arts organizations, the museums, the Metropoli-
tan, and so on and so on, probably the Library of Congress—I
don't know your history in this regard—have grabbed off im-
mense amounts of money, relatively. One of the shocking things
we discovered was, of the 33 million-some-odd annual budget of
the New York State Arts Council, exactly one-sixty-fourth of that
amount of money went to literature. This seems to me dispropor-
tionate. And therefore the scale of the proposal is a very important part of it. I'm reminded of the time—'69, I believe—when
the Swedish museum director Pontus Hultén was given the direc-
torship of the Moderna Museet in Sweden, and he went to the
Swedish Parliament, and he asked for 30 million kroner, and they
were shocked and astounded. This was ten times the amount that
a director had ever asked for before. So they gave him 15 million
kroner, which was five times the amount the museum had ever
had before. It's the same strategy. We're keeping our fingers
crossed; we hope it's going to work.

Randolph:

You know, of course, Donald, that the entire Literature Program budget at the National Endowment for the Arts this year was 1.9 million.

Barthelme:

Get to work. You get to work.

Kathleen Fraser:

Well, I became a writer because I had a great deal of trouble speaking. And then I begged to come in front of Donald, but no, we had to go in alphabetical order, it's an odd position. I don't want to talk, really, as a former director of the Poetry Center, because one of the reasons I left a job that I cared about very much and chose to give an enormous amount of energy to was in order to survive as a writer. And I'm feeling, at this conference, very much in the frustrating position of being a poet whose first two books were published by Kayak Press, a small press in California. My first book was George Hitchcock's first book. I was a naive, just-out-of-college person in New York—actually, it was three years after that—after having studied with Stanley Kunitz. George had never done books, but he had done a few issues of a magazine. I was interested in the photo-offset process and the way that he could use graphics and interesting paper and I didn't feel that I was all ready to do a large official New York book. But I wrote to him, and really in a very naive way or I wouldn't have been able to do it, and asked him if he might be interested, and he said, "If it amuses you, send me a manuscript." And I did, and he decided to do a book, and that was the beginning of Kayak Books. And he subsequently published a number of people, including Phil Levine, and just many, many American poets, and did a second book of mine together with graphics by Judy Starbuck, which was again for me a very beautiful experience of combining graphics and poetry. And because I'm a visual person, it meant a great deal. And there was just a lot of—a sense of working together with someone and that process that happens in small-press publishing. My third book was of a different sort—not photo-offset, but a small press begun by a woman in Iowa, whom I'd never met, who wrote to me and said she wanted to start a book-printing little establishment of her own. She's into fine printing and making really beautiful, rare books. Her name is Bonnie O'Connell, and she does Penumbra Press. This is the kind of thing where, instead of sending out to a small but well-distributed kind of thing such as George Hitchcock established, Bonnie sent out invitations. And this was a very special way of having a book done. It was a beautiful gift, to have a book done in this way. But on the other hand, it was not really accessible to a large number of people. Only the people who were on that particular invitation list even knew about it, except for rare book collectors and certain librarians.

Okay, this sort of went through a period of years, and then Fran McCullough at Harper & Row invited me to give her a manuscript, and this was after I had been writing for quite a while. And I still didn't feel quite ready to do that, but a couple years went by and then I did feel ready. And that book was a collection that included poems from the first three small-press books. Fran I don't think would have been interested if it hadn't been for those early books, since, because of those books, I was able to give a reading in New York, where Fran heard me read. What I'm trying to describe is a slow building process of a very shy poet who wouldn't have had whatever it takes to go out there and push for a big book. But I was able to do it in little stages, and I am deeply grateful to each of the people behind these books, and I feel very torn by the very real differences that are holding the established publishing world and the small-press coterie world apart, because my heart is with both. I couldn't possibly give all my loyalty to one or the other. I feel an enormous amount of joy and energy with the small-press people who were talking. I feel I want to be with that energy of seeking out a very meaningful audience for work, to have one's book go to people who are hungry for it. On the other hand, a big book reaches people that you simply don't know about, and it goes into libraries—a much larger range of libraries—and is available just simply on a completely different scale. So the things that really attracted me through the various talks that people have given have been very practical kinds of things. I loved Galen's list idea, and I very much liked David Godine's quite particular ideas about how he was thinking about distribution and promotion and taking as seriously those aspects of poetry books as well as fiction or nonfiction. I liked what Dan Halpern said. I was paying a lot of attention to the particular qualities of the development, again, of reaching an audience. My fear is that these things all sort of went by and that everyone agreed and nodded heads. And I have been wishing for a place to bring these very practical technical kinds of questions and possible resolutions together.

So I would like to informally propose the possibility of thinking about doing a project. It might be through one particular paid person or an organization such as Poets & Writers, which tends so beautifully to all the practical problems that poets and new prose writers seem unable to cope with. Anyway, a technological project

and enough money to pay for it—I'm not asking you, Leonard—
to approach specific people who have been here, who have mentioned real lists and real processes of promotion. Now, I asked
Dan Halpern specifically about his list that he prepared for Viking. He went to a great deal of trouble to develop this list himself. He has an arrangement with them. They put it on the computer, so they went to a lot of expense to do it. In their businesslike way, they don't want to share it with anyone. That's par for
the course. I'm sure that there must be fifty companies, large and
small, who feel that way—that kind of territorial protection of the
list. I think somehow that has to be broken down if we really, in
good faith, care about developing a larger audience for poetry. If
it means that there has to be a bit of funding for buying lists, then
that has to be done, I suppose. I think that small presses are just
as snobby and territorial or protective of their lists. Some of my
friends that are involved in the small-press business like the idea
of having a very, very exclusive list, and only we of the underground, who really understand this particular kind of poetry,
would be interested in reading this kind of thing, anyway. I really
question that. I know that during the last two years, because of a
subscription to *Psychology Today* at one point, I was put on some
incredible list that then went to a number of magazines. And I
started receiving glorious brochures on this and that, and I ended
up getting subscriptions, out of sheer curiosity, to the Smithsonian
Institution magazine, and to *Scientific American,* and things that I
normally might not have just gone out and ordered a subscription
to. I found that I was curious when they told me about the content. I found there were things, yes, I did want to read them,
even if only in terms of exploring language. And now I'm reading
these magazines and looking at them, and I think that this potential is there in any list that's brought together.

Okay. After lists comes a way of developing publicity. This is
another problem for people who are shy and don't feel like being
performers. I don't mean giving readings, but I mean having
somehow, to get your book around, to have to make an image for
yourself, and go out and somehow package it and sell it and appear on Johnny Carson or whatever! It just doesn't go along with
a lot of personalities, at least that are involved in poetry, and it
seems a shame that that is the only way to do it. Now, I know that
when I received, from Dan's list, a notice of Louise Glück's book,
I thought it was very nicely done; it was a one-page brochure with
a picture and the price of the book and a few comments, and it
was done tastefully. It wasn't a hard-sell thing, and yet it notified
me and all the other people on the list. And I think it's a very real
way of reaching people. This is the kind of information that I

would like to be brought together in a specific project. I want to pin it down for the future—you know, this is your future—and to bring in people as consultants, such as David Godine, people who were here at this conference, to pool the information.

I'd just like to tell about one tiny project in California, and that's a new thing called Inkslingers, which is another way of promoting interest in books. This is a group of small-press people who are into poetry, small-press editions, printing, doing their own printing, making their own papers and graphics. And they're getting together and trying to develop ways of getting grass-roots interest in writing, in local writers. They're trying to find ways of connecting with local librarians and developing lists and ways of showing the work of local printers. I think this is very important and it's something that could be worked on and developed on a more national scale.

Thank you.

Randolph:

Betty Kray.

Elizabeth Kray:

I've always thought that composers and writers should get together, because composers have been doing this sort of thing for years and years. They've had cooperatives, they've been putting out records, they have printed their own scores. They're doing very well indeed. And I've never understood why writers and composers just simply don't share facilities. I think they could. My husband edited for a number of years a magazine called *New Music.* It's the idea of the magazine that it would only print scores that had been rejected. And the magazine now reads like a *Who's Who.* It's incredible.

I am not talking about composers, I am really talking about libraries. I am restricting myself to small libraries in Rhode Island. I live part-time in Rhode Island. I live a lot in New York. And everything that I say about small libraries in Rhode Island could apply to branch libraries in New York, because a branch serves a neighborhood and a community and a specific kind of people. But it's, in a sense, more romantic to talk about small-town libraries. And I'm out on a limb in Rhode Island. Last week, I talked to sixty librarians in Westerly, Rhode Island, about a poetry program that they should put into effect. The reason for this was that the resource librarian for the region—the region is called South County, which stretches from Providence to the

Connecticut border—had invested $100 in poetry books. I talked her into it. Secondly, I talked her into having Nancy Sullivan— who lives in Rhode Island, who's published by David Godine, who's a poet—go with the librarian to buy the books. I'd noticed that librarians have a tendency to think in terms of gimmicks—I mean the resource librarian was all for buying women's poetry at that moment, because she thought that would attract people. And of course she bought a lot of books by women, there's no doubt about that, but by other people too. But now she has spent $100 in paperback poetry books for a whole series of small-town librar- ies, and I'm absolutely responsible. I've absolutely promised to help her and the assembled librarians in the Westerly library to work out some way in which we could get people to read some of those books. Again, I would like to say that in talking to them we did mention fine fiction, not only poetry. We just brought poetry, but we talked to them about a collection of, I suppose you might even say those old-fashioned words, belles lettres.

I'd like to say something else at this moment and then go back to the program that we're in the process of working out—with absolutely no money, by the way. And that's that libraries, small libraries, maybe a lot of other libraries, too, are an endangered species. I don't know if any of you have read the National Com- mission on Libraries' report. It's a report put together by a lot of distinguished and fine-minded people, but it scares me to death. Throughout, there's a discussion of the need to make libraries into telecommunications centers. It talks a lot about data banks. It talks about the necessity of being able to flash information from a research library on the East Coast to one in the West, and so forth. These things are very necessary, and it's good to have tech- nology used properly, that's splendid. But what worried me throughout this was the fact that here was being worked up, here was being projected an idea of a systematic library system all working together, and throughout the word used was *informa- tion*. It seemed to me that I didn't see the word *knowledge*—yes, *knowledge* was used, indeed it was, but it seemed to me that those two words were used interchangeably, and I've always thought there was a great big difference between them. And that's a really scary thing. And that is one of the reasons I'm interested in small libraries, because they are diversified. They do serve the commun- ities. I did find something at Westerly that was very touching. An old librarian told me in the township of Hopkinton they have two libraries. And it's sort of an extravagance, but they're keeping these two libraries going so that children can walk to them. And I think that's an extraordinarily important thing, to have children be able to walk to a library. Anyhow, that's kind of a digression.

Now I want to go back to something: the reasons why librari-

ans don't buy poetry, and why, to invest $100 into a poetry collec-
tion, we have to have Nancy go down with this very well-meaning
and very intelligent woman, and help her. Librarians don't read
reviews. And they don't read reviews because they don't trust
them, and they don't trust reviews because reviews don't tell them
anything. Reviews are written for friends, I'm afraid, on the
whole. They're written by friends for a certain group of people.
Reviews talk a very intimate language. They don't say one word to
the librarian. She does not know, after reading a review of praise,
why the book is praised, what it's praised for, and whether or not
to buy it. She has no way of distinguishing between one book
that's praised and another book that's praised. She has reason to
distrust, sometimes, a panning review, so she doesn't buy poetry.
We have—by we, I mean the academy—put out booklists, and you
probably have all received them. Librarians use them as much as
they can. There's a young woman in our office, Susan Mernett, a
young poet, whose pride it is to include every book published in
the United States. I suppose she might miss one or two.
Librarians use these books, go through them as checklists, and
university librarians find them extremely useful. But a librarian in
a small public library system doesn't really know much. They're
just titles to that person.

So one of the things I propose to do for the librarians of Rhode
Island is to have reviews prepared for them. And some of the
poets, some of my friends, are writing these reviews and they're
doing it for nothing. We want to have a little collection of them.
We want to see what the form is that is most helpful. These reviews are very short, just a paragraph. They're reviewing a book.
The librarian will have some sense of what the book is. We're
going to have it on a card that she'll be able to file and use if
some kid comes in who's really interested in poetry. The readers'
guide service: that's a person, that's not a reference book. There
is a readers' guide woman in the small libraries, and it's a service
she performs; people come and talk to her about their needs.

We're also going to do all those other things that one does.
We're going to have readings. In some of the little towns, we're
going to try to hook the people by having anthology readings to
reacquaint a lot of people who stopped reading poetry when they
left college, having a few familiar names for them, and then working them in with newer poets. We have a whole program. My time
is up, and I'm just going to stop right now.

Barbara Ringer:

When I first saw the title of this panel, my reaction was to wonder what I was doing on it, because my field is copyright, and that

certainly has a lot to do with the survival of the author, but it doesn't have to do much with support by organizations and foundations. In fact, my feeling is that the two are inconsistent and that perhaps the survival of the writer and support by organizations and foundations are inconsistent. That is my theme.

Copyright was described by Ernest Newman in his biography of Richard Wagner as "those incredible laws written by parliaments of fools for the benefit of knaves." I think that perhaps we've gotten past that point. He was describing bad copyright laws, and I'm not sure that all copyright laws need to be bad. But when I think about the title of this panel, I'm wondering if it shouldn't be subtitled, "Will You Walk into My Parlor? Said the Spider to the Fly," or perhaps worse yet, "Put Out the Light and Then Put Out the Light." If I shake anybody up, I hope I do.

There are quite a few bad copyright laws, and the little number we're operating under, which goes back to 1909, is one of the worst. It's been under attack; there have been consistent efforts to change it since 1926. It was enacted in 1909, and it was archaic then. It was not only archaic, but it was stingy and unjust to writers. And the efforts to reform it did not originate with writers. They originated with users, the people who exploit writers. And I think that this is a tragic situation. We have a bill in Congress now, which I'm rather hopeful for. Among other things, it will, I think, perhaps bring the author up to 1909, where he should have been then. I don't think it goes much further than that, and the hassling over it is in the big-money issues. And meanwhile, the writer's survival is going down the drain. I'll be glad to answer any questions at the end, or perhaps even after the end, about the bill and what it contains, but I'd like to look at this from a larger, broader, longer-range point of view. I'd like to regard copyright not as the act of 1909 and not as the right to collect royalties or the exclusive right to sue a cable company or something like that, but as the legal condition of authorship, the whole schmier. Considered this way, copyright is as old as the writing profession and will last as long as there is any creativity left in the human race.

When people talk about the possibility of copyright ceasing to exist, they're referring to traditional legal systems under which authors are given exclusive rights and presumably get royalties in exchange for licensing them. Obviously, this system has broken down, and I think that's what this whole panel and seminar is about. It's being engulfed not by economics but by technology. And copyright in the broad sense has already begun to change. Whatever emerges is still going to be copyrighted in the sense of the way that a society chooses to protect its creative people, but it could be something that would be horrible to contemplate.

I'd like to take as my reference point a rather short passage from John Wain's biography of Samuel Johnson that was published earlier this year—and he charted out two centuries, which we are well beyond by now. He called it "the era of the triangle." He pointed out that when Johnson began his profession in the 1730s or thereabouts—the second quarter of the eighteenth century—the age of patronage had ended. And the only authors who were able to survive, really, were those who wrote partisan pieces for newspapers and anonymous political propaganda. And the condition of true authorship during this era was monstrous. The author was utterly defenseless and vulnerable. He said: "The age of munificent patronage, of well-paid government posts going automatically to men of literary reputation, had faded almost over the horizon; the new daylight, that of the direct relationship of author and public, was yet no more than a dapple in the sky." This "new daylight" coincided with the legal recognition of authors' rights as distinguished from government rights and publishers' rights.

The first copyright law in the world was enacted during this era, in 1710 in England. The second copyright law followed our revolution, first in the states during the Articles of Confederation period and later was recognized in the Constitution itself. And the third was in revolutionary France. This system, which was in existence for two hundred years, and a lot of people seem to think it's still going on, he refers to as the triangle: ". . . that tringle of author, publisher and reader which gave a shape to literary endeavor from the middle of the eighteenth century to the middle of the twentieth, when it collapsed again into a chaos of subsidiary rights and complicated side deals."

He thus puts a fence around these two centuries. This was preceded by the era of patronage; his golden age was the age of the triangle. What we are now in is the age of, he would say, the subsidiary right and the side deal, or the age of the media, if you want to use our awful jargon. In his words, "This was the era in which the author spoke directly to the reader through the publisher." And you have probably had some publishers here who don't realize this yet, but this has collapsed. They are not a viable third side of the triangle. In fact the triangle has ceased to exist.

We are now in an era of chaos for authors, and the reasons lie with the revolutionary changes in communications technology and the failure of the copyright law to keep pace with the needs of authorship in the new era. In other words, the reason for the author's plight is not that the government and the Ford Foundation and the fat-cat corporations have not been pumping enough money into authorship and the arts. The reason is the failure of the copyright law, which is the legal framework of authorship, to

keep pace with the technological challenge. The answer, in my
opinion, is not to get the government and the fat cats to pump
money into authorship, but to restore the author as a viable wage
earner in the sense that he has been for the past two hundred
years.

It almost seems superfluous to observe that the technological
revolution in communications is a pivotal event in the history of
mankind and that its full impact has not yet been felt at all. I don't
have a clue as to which of the electronic marvels will prove to be
transitory toys and gadgets and which, if any, will turn out to be
something like the monolith in Clark's *2001*. I am sure—and I
think most of us here are, too—that amid all this electronics, the
quality of human life is changing. And I have been terribly frightened by the implications of satellites. If I were going to pick
something out, I would pick that out.

But think about what's happened since 1909, when the law that
you're operating under, that you're writing under, was written. I
can just run them down, very fast: motion pictures, radio, television, cable, pay television, computers, satellites, and audio and
video tape recording, photocopy, microreprography, and the au-
tomation of the composition and production of printed matter of
various sorts, which I think has had more impact than people realize. This does not exhaust the list at all, and many of these developments combine and interact, providing nationwide and
worldwide networks for all this business. You have information
and misinformation, culture and kitsch, entertainment and stupor,
propaganda and personal gratification. And there is evidently no
end to this descent into the maelstrom.

Many people still regard this as an unqualified blessing. I think
of the people Betty was talking about in the NCLIS library report,
and so on. They are eager to press on, eyes ablaze, to buy all the
new machinery they can afford in building their own particular
bridges over their own particular River Kwai. Maybe it's too soon
to judge the situation fairly. We are pretty close to it, but I can't
see that all this machinery has produced much except a craving
for more machinery. Education and literacy are currently on a
downhill plunge. Wider access to information seems to result in
people being less and less informed about more and more. Scholarship and research, which were once based on reading and note-
taking, now seem to consist of accumulating filing cabinets full of
unread Xerox copies.

I am not foolish enough to think that this whole relentless process can be reversed or halted or even slowed by anything except
lack of money. And that's temporary, at least in the government.
The pendulum swings. But I do think that if we could pause long
enough to examine what we're doing to ourselves we might be

able to establish some control over the development of technology for its own sake, to channel it better, and to rethink the problem in purely human terms. I am all in favor of opening up new avenues for creative endeavor, like the invention of new painting techniques and musical instruments during the Renaissance. The inventions of the past few decades have brought about a new breed of creators throughout the whole range of the arts, and they have allowed people who were incapable of fixing their creative endeavors, like singers and instrumentalists, to provide permanency for their creations and to get a much broader audience. But at the same time I think the era of the media has wounded or destroyed some traditional forms of expression, has sent some truly gifted artists off on fools' errands, and has produced an increasingly glutted, tasteless, and bored audience. A lot more people are making a lot more money out of the arts and letters in the United States now than did in 1909. And some valuable tools and creative outlets have sprung into existence since then. But what has happened to the traditional authors of the era of the triangle, the ones we are here talking about—the novelist, the playwright, the poet, the short-story writer, and the whole range of historians, composers, essayists, critics, and so forth?

The third side of the triangle has collapsed. It started to collapse for them about 1950, which happens to be when television made its big breakthrough in America. With few exceptions, traditional authors in 1975 cannot make a living from their profession any more. They've always had to struggle, but it's really almost literally impossible now. To write at all, they increasingly must go into service to the big corporations, the big government, or the educational bureaucrats. To a greater or lesser degree, the bureaucrats control the use of their time, the content of their works, and the manner in which their works are disseminated. If authors choose to write independently, they must often push their way through a mob of hucksters, lawyers, and machines to reach a dwindling public, and that public, of course, is now spending half its waking hours watching dots dancing on a little tube.

Assuming an author's work makes its way into print, in something resembling the form in which it was written, what danger does it next encounter? Well, it encounters photocopying, among other things, and no longer just a page or two. It is now apparent that more and more libraries are reluctant to let copies from their collections off the premises. Instead of performing their traditional lending services, libraries are purveying neatly bound or slip-cased photocopies free of cost or at cost. Interlibrary loan may still be interlibrary, but it has certainly ceased to be loan. And photocopying as it is practiced in 1975 is only a passing phase. Automatic hard-copy retrieval from cathode-ray tube displays of microform images is already upon us, and so are worldwide tele-communications facilities to transmit those images hither and yon.

There is a clearcut historical trend in copyright law, and I will not go into the details. I'm afraid that Len felt that I was going to give you a real zippy rundown on what renewal of copyright involves, but that is something else again. The trend is compulsory licensing, where the author gets money but loses control, and every time a new medium comes along, the attack of the user is based on, "I'm willing to pay, but I am not willing to give up my right to free access." We will have, probably, if we get this bill through Congress, about four compulsory licenses and maybe five in it. Also, these compulsory licenses for new media are beginning to expand into the old traditional forms of authorship and expression. And there are very great dangers in this. If authors are not smart enough to organize themselves somehow, and co-ops may not be enough—collectives may be necessary of one sort or other—you're going to force them to write for hire in one way or another. And of course they don't have any control then. And even if they can get government money, there is a big school of thought, as Leonard knows very well, that says, "Well, hell, if the government is spending the money on it, then the public ought to have it free, it ought to be available without any proprietary rights at all." And this is a very insistent, populist creed, believe me. What we've got is a very ugly picture, and, in terms of copyright and the condition of the individual author, one can read the signs with genuine despair. But there is some slap-happy optimism out there at the same time. There are people who mindlessly push government or corporate patronage of authors with one hand and push the substitution of the machines for culture with the other.

I am fairly confident that the bill we've got in Congress now is going to go through next year, and it will lay the conditions for authorship for the next quarter century, perhaps. There will probably be, as I said, four or five forms of compulsory licensing. Assuming that technology continues its relentless march, the demands for compulsory licensing will continue to grow. Unless they are matched by countervailing demands to protect the individual and personal rights of authors, the era of the media will give way to a new era of patronage, but one in which the patrons are not going to be the rich and the aristocratic, but instead are going to be the bureaucrats who run the corporations, the foundations, or the state. Government control over all aspects of authorship is a real possibility in the twenty-first century. And if this happens, we will have no one but ourselves to blame.

It is not enough merely to avert this danger, real as it is. As history teaches, it is quite possible for a rich culture to flourish, even under a tyrannical system. But Orwell foresaw that sometime, perhaps in the 1980s, the combination of tyranny and technocracy could destroy not only freedom of expression and the quality of life but human culture itself. No patron, government or otherwise, ever paid out money to support artists or anybody else without getting something in return. If authors let their copyrights erode and expect uncle to provide, they are in for a terrible surprise. And if the users of the new communications technologies insist on using authors' works without giving some appropriate compensation in return, they will find that sooner or later there will be no authors worth reading and no works worth reproducing.

The author's appropriate compensation is his copyright, and it cannot be limited to money or to fame or to tenure in a university. Ultimately, it must consist of independence, the freedom to write as one believes, and to find people to communicate with. A bad copyright law can destroy that independence; a good one can help to preserve it.

Thank you.

Randolph:

Grace.

Grace Schulman:

If I speak briefly about the past, it is because the future depends on it. The Poetry Center of the 92d Street YM-YWHA is one of the oldest public platforms for spoken poetry. It began thirty-seven years ago and has since then presented some of the major poets of this century as well as new writers of four decades.

Although poetry has always been a spoken art, the spoken form gained new significance early in the century, after 1912, when Ezra Pound admonished poets to compose in the sequence of the musical phrase, not in the sequence of the metronome. For many of those new poets, patterns of corresponding stresses determined the structures of their freer verse, which was marked by a natural conversational flow and whose rhythm was not dictated by meter or end-rhyme. For that reason and others, poetry had to be read aloud. That became even more urgent in the thirties with the advent of tape recorders and records, when such poets as Marianne Moore said—Marianne Moore actually said that she revised many of her poems from syllabic to free verse when she heard herself read aloud on records for the first time.

In the late 1960s, sadly, the Poetry Center had to present fewer readings than before and presented, instead, lectures by architects, scientists, and anthropologists, on the assumption that the

Poetry Center's pioneer role was over. Readings were being given throughout New York as well as the United States, the world. And the reason for this change was to bring in an additional source of revenue. The Poetry Center was losing about $500 on each reading. After a few years, however, these nonpoetry programs were losing money as well and no longer helped to defray the cost of poetry readings.

When I was appointed director of the Poetry Center in March 1974, I said that I believed in the urgency of poetry readings in our time because of the sense of community they provide. I sent a letter to more than two hundred poets asking them not what poets they felt deserved to read at the Poetry Center but what poets they would actually leave their homes to hear. I added that the question went beyond my poems and theirs and beyond the poems of our friends and students. We invited the poets they asked to hear, and last season we had twenty-five poetry readings of around forty-five poets. They included poets from abroad, such as Octavio Paz, Ernesto Cardinale, Yehuda Amichai; established poets, such as Richard Wilbur, Robert Penn Warren, and Stanley Kunitz. We had neglected wonderful poets, such as Robert Francis, Madeline DeFrees, Harvey Shapiro; and newer poets, such as Louise Glück, Marilyn Hacker. The audience turnout was gratifying. From 200 to 600 people—600 for the night of Octavio Paz—came to most events in the autumn of 1974. Although we tried to plan smaller events for the spring of 1975 when the Kaufman Auditorium was temporarily closed for repair and we had to use the art gallery, several readings were so well attended that we had to place more than 200 seats in a gallery that held only 150.

Still, we are losing more money than it is feasible to lose. Steps are being taken to make up for the loss, and, at the same time, promote the coordination of printed poetry with poetry reading. This season we started a new series of records of the Poetry Center in coordination with Caedmon Records, having discovered an archive of great recorded readings that were not being used by scholars or for profit in some years. This new series—it's not really a new series, it's a continuation of the old one that stopped some time ago—will include the old masters who read at the Y and contemporary poets as well.

The new Baruch College Poetry Series presents poets who are currently reading at the Y. We started that series—it's at the college where I teach—to give my students an opportunity to meet the poets and also to provide an additional source of publicity and of money for poets who come to New York to read at the Y.

We have merged the Discovery contest, the traditional competition for poets whose work has not been published in book form, with the *Nation,* and now it is called Discovery—*The Nation.*

Each of the four winning poets has at least one poem printed in a special issue of the *Nation,* which is distributed on the evening of the Discovery program. And, of course, this includes publicity for the contest earlier than the night itself.

We have instituted more poetry workshops led by teachers who have a variety of different strengths. Since they are a source of revenue and because we believe in the education of readers as well as of young people who want to be poets, we have, of course, exploited all possibilities of publicity, particularly at campuses, at colleges throughout the city and nearby.

Still, the costs of presenting these readings have risen sharply. I'm very glad that our current season consists of fourteen poetry readings with twenty-eight fine new and established writers. I am concerned that there are only fourteen evenings, rather than twenty-four or thirty-four. There are many good writers today, and their voices must be heard. I hope that the future will bring more poetry to the Poetry Center, but I cannot promise there will be more in these bleak times.

Randolph:

Galen, you're on last.

Galen Williams:

I'm an anal-compulsive, and I do like lists, and I liked Kathy's idea. I think that there should be some step toward trying to gather these in the next year. I'm also not a writer, so I don't have a conflict. I can devote a lot of time to gathering names, and one of the things that came out of it very early was with Leonard's support. We kept gathering names from the time that I was at the Y, with Betty's help, and requests coming from all over the nation, seeing our ads in the *Times:* "How can we get hold of this writer, that writer?" We just started keeping files and telephone Roll-a-dexes, and we finally worked that into a list of about 800 names and addresses. And we typed it up, Leonard ran it off, and then that was just a mimeographed list. Then we found 500 more poets we just never knew about, through friends. We got up to 1,200 and then, this past year, finally published, again, with NEA's help, this *Directory of American Poets,* which is about 1,550 names—about one-fifth are minority writers and about a third are women—and there's a lot more out there, we know. We have panel systems that keep processing, going through new names, and each panel passes maybe 150 names twice a year. We then were able to establish a body of research for fiction writers, and the *Directory* is coming out in January. There are about 800 and some fiction writers in the *Directory*. It will be the first *Directory*, though, so I don't know if there are several hundred more fiction writers out there who will then be, I hope, contacting our office in New York saying, "Let me be part of the next one." The *Directory* after that will be a combined poets' and fiction writers' directory, so finally we'll have everything all under one cover, which will be more efficient.

The *Directory*, though, is soon out of date, because one-third of the authors' list keeps changing every year. They're very peripatetic. We had to invent a system to update the *Directory* regularly, and Leonard gave us a "rump" grant in our first year. The first issue was eight pages, and the last issue, the most recent one, which is a newsletter now called *Coda,* is thirty-two pages. It started out as the supplement, but it's ended up as a newsletter, with investigative reporting, listings of grants where you can get more money, administrators who want to hire poets, poets and fiction writers who are making trips from other parts of the country and want to read on the East Coast from the West—anything we can think of that is not biased that will help get cash into a poet's pocket through information. The issue before that was on writers' colonies. We realized that a lot of writers didn't know about any of the colonies except Yaddo or MacDowell. And there turned out to be twelve which we discovered. Since then, there are four more who have written us, and we'll publish them in subsequent issues. *Coda* will now come out on a subscription basis, five dollars a year for five issues. We'll have two supplements a year, updating each of the directories, which will go to all purchasers of the *Directory*. We've developed quite accurate lists over the last two years. We have about twenty-seven hundred writers—twenty-six hundred writers, poets, and fiction writers, about five hundred administrators around the nation, and we often get calls from writers and publishers saying, "How can we help promote our author?" And in this *Directory* and fiction directory as well, there's a whole section, broken down by state, with a map that shows who the administrators are all over the nation. So that either the poets can make up brochures and mail them themselves or they can rent our sponsors list, at very minimal cost, and send out their mailing through the addressograph system, so that they don't have to address them all by hand.

There was one more point on tours. Oh, well. I'll remember and come back to it, on how to promote your tours.

Beyond that, through the New York State Arts Council, we have helped get cash into the poets' pockets in a little mini-WPA program, by helping to supplement fees for readings, such as the readings at the `˙ʼ` or the Academy of American Poets in New York, but all over the state. And we spent $80,000 last year getting money to writers—$80,000 got to writers. Many of our grants are matching grants, and we raised $60,000 additionally for writers, so through this program, $140,000 got into writers' pockets. And there's lots more out there, all over New York State, and Leonard has started a program for the whole nation this coming year, where you're distributing—is it $100,000?

Randolph:

Yes.

Williams:

For all the states, so every state can have a poet or a fiction writer or a playwright, and have him be supplemented, which is a very good trick, because administrators think, "Oh if I have $100, and I get another $100, I'll do the reading."

Grace mentioned that the Y had to cut down on poetry readings. But we supported four hundred writers—we didn't support them, we got money to four hundred different writers with the $80,000, which is one hundred more than last year. Of these writers, 80 percent were poets and the rest were fiction writers and some playwrights. So, this morning there was a point about fiction writers, but Ed Doctorow goes out for $200, $300, even though he's now best-seller. In fact, he said he didn't want to take the state money this time because he doesn't charge too much, he's a wonderful reader. Donald is too. Thirty-five percent of these four hundred writers were women, and 14 percent were minority writers. And the span of support goes from Jane Cortez, who is a black writer, who was supported fifteen times; Spencer Holst, who is a fiction writer, a storyteller, thirteen times; Neil Baldwin, who is a not-too-well-known poet up in Buffalo, twelve times—he got what Betty was talking about, a community interest. A lot of people in that community wanted him in different situations. We support that. Lyn Lifshin and David Ignatow each were supported eleven times; Galway Kinnell, Muriel Rukeyser, and Kenneth Koch, nine times. So you don't have to be famous to get this support. And about 250 different organizations around New York State used our service. They got this money, which was from one hundred different communities. So the span can happen, just multiplying in snowball effect all over the nation.

The other thing I was going to mention about *Coda* is that we're opening it up to ads in the February issue, because we have this list of eight thousand people whom we think are prime targets for poetry readings, for poetry books, and fine fiction. If a publisher doesn't want to rent our lists, which are more expensive,

of course, than running an ad, he can just do the ad and see what
effect it has. And writers' publishers can rent our lists, too, if they
want. It's all broken down by state and by sponsor and by—even
our complimentary list, which is a very good publicity list. Kathy
asked about a publicity list. We took the COSMEP list and expanded on it, and I'd say it's a very good basic list for donation.

Randolph:

Before we open up to questions from the floor, I'd like to make
one slight response to something Barbara said. First of all, I agree
wholeheartedly with the thrust of what you were saying. I think
that the so-called electronic era is probably the most frightening
thing that's ever happened to private creativity and to the private
control of private interest. And I doubt seriously, unless some
major steps are taken, that genuine copyright, the genuine protection of the writer's rights, may disappear, as Barbara says, by the
beginning of the next century, anyway.

However, I think that, in one regard—and I'm emphasizing as
things now stand, where the endowment's fellowships are concerned, and this applies only to the fellowships in the Endowment
for the Arts, it does not apply to other things—when a writer
makes an application for a fellowship to the Literature Program at
the National Endowment for the Arts, it is clearly understood that
if that writer is given a fellowship, the fellowship is given just to
buy the writer time, to give him or her a chance to travel or to
purchase materials. There is no project necessary, and we do not
want a product in exchange. All we ask for is a one-page or a
one-paragraph final report when the grant period is over, and we
do not want anything to do with whatever product is created as a
result of that fellowship. The same thing is true with the small-
press grants. The very simple reason for that, I think, Barbara
made that rather clear in what she was saying. I have a very personal aversion to the idea of the government owning anything
that any artist creates, unless it commissions it directly for a painting or something like that, and that's a different matter. I think
that there is danger, always, whenever the government at any level is involved with the work of a private creative individual. I
think, however, a lot of the fear that was evident before the endowment's legislation was passed in 1965 has been alleviated by
the history of the past ten years, thanks to people like Carolyn
Kizer, Roger Stevens, Nancy Hanks, Michael Straight, Brian
O'Dougherty, and a lot of other people who have been on the
staff there. And I emphasize that what I'm saying is that, as things
now stand, I think we're in good shape. I hope we go on being
that way forever. I hope the endowment does, anyway.

All right. We'd like to open it up to questions from the floor.
We do have time. Last night we didn't get out of here until almost
five o'clock, so we've got quite a bit of time. No questions? Good
Lord, everybody thought you were going to be the audience that's
going to ask the most.

Williams:

Leonard, could I ask Barbara Ringer a question? I'm not sure
that I understand exactly what compulsory licensing means.

Randolph:

I'm not sure Barbara can explain it in the next forty-five minutes.

Ringer:

Well, you have an almost predictable process that goes on when
new technological developments hit the copyright fan. The first is
that the technology just goes right ahead, nobody stops it, and
money is invested, and there is a success. Then somebody suddenly gets nervous about copyright, and you look at the 1909 law,
and it isn't clear. So you go on, but a little nervously, using the
medium. Then, sooner or later, somebody sues, and you get to the
point where the courts, which used to say, up to 1950, "All right,
the 1909 law, when it said *perform,* really meant *broadcast."*
After 1950, no more. Reproduction does not necessarily mean photocopying, and performing does not mean cablecasting—cable re-
transmission. In other words, the courts say, "Gee, we've got a big
technology going here, and we can't stop it. And they say they
can't really pay, so we're not going to cut it off. It's up to Congress to do its duty." So the thing goes to the congressional arena,
and in the congressional arena congressmen have very high-
priced lobbyists beating on them, and they are conscious of the
political consequences of what they're going to do. So what happens? They compromise. And the compromise inevitably is going
to be, "Okay, author, we will pay you. Okay, publisher, if you're
in the picture, we will pay you. But we can't allow you to withhold
the work from this new medium that is proceeding to go forward,
lickety-split." So the new medium gets access under what is a
compulsory license, in the sense that the author, or the copyright
owner to whom he may have transferred his rights, has a right to
compensation. But he must compulsorily transfer the right to
users under certain conditions, which are spelled out in the stat-
ute. And I say, I really don't want to pursue this subject down to
its depths, but you've always got the government involved, because

you're going to have a pie with money, and it's got to be split up somehow. And even if you don't—as many of the compulsory licensing provisions of the new bill do—have the government setting the rates, having some kind of a tribunal which has "Czar" written all over it, if you don't have that sort of thing dividing up, setting the rates, at least you've got it dividing up the money. And when you've got to come to a government agency to get your money, then you cede some of your freedom. There's no question about this in my mind.

Randolph:

Let me mention one thing about the copyright, or the rights to works, which I think you'll find interesting, too, Barbara. This past year, in conjunction with the Ford Foundation, the Corporation for Public Broadcasting, the Public Media Program of the National Endowment for the Arts in cooperation with the Literature Program made a grant to public television station KCET in Los Angeles, for the commissioning and production of a series of original plays by contemporary American writers who had not previously written for television or film or radio. These are all writers who had not been involved in the media before. One of the provisions of the contract we signed with Barbara Schultz, who is the overall producer, is that the rights to the scripts revert to the writers at the end of three years—all of them. Any further use of that script from then on belongs to the writer. That's the first time that's ever happened, and it's a good precedent. Both Chloe Aaron, who is director of Public Media, and I worked on that for a period of the better part of three months, convincing the Ford Foundation and CPB and KCET that this was really what they ought to do. But it is an interesting precedent. Clayton, you had a question.

Eshleman:

Yes. I wanted to ask both Kathleen and Galen to follow up this idea about the lists. In other words, if you could get people to cooperate and you could build up a list, a combined list-list, what functional use do you think could be made of it?

Fraser:

Well, first of all, I think that once it's compiled, the availability of it should be known, should be announced in something like *Coda* of Poets & Writers. And any group of editors that is known about in the publishing companies that exist and in the small-press lists that exist should have this available to them as a

kind of list that can be used to notify people of new books coming
out. The irony of doing a book with a big company like Harper &
Row, for instance, is that you are working with a very good editor,
say, whom you really trust and with whom you have a fine relationship. And then the book goes through a lot of other processes, a lot of almost mechanical, huge processes, and pretty soon
there's not that connection that an intimate press has. You feel, if
you're a new writer, comparatively speaking, "How am I going to
reach an audience, a meaningful audience?" A lot of big publishers don't have that contact. I'm just amazed by the fact of the
bigness of it, and all this equipment that's available, all this technology that's terrifying, and yet it's not used in any practical way
to help new writers to meet audiences. It's always pushed off on
the fact that they have no money to put into publicity for new
writers, you know, unless it's a nonfiction or. . . .

Williams:

Yesterday, there was so much talk about no audience out there
for even a giveaway book. If there were going to be purchase
programs started in this country, as Leonard has begun on a small
term and the New York State Arts Council has done, you buy five
hundred copies of a book, and then you don't know whom to
send it to. This could be the basis of a book club. You would poll
your readers or your people on your list and ask who would like
this book. At least you have a name to send it to.

Randolph:

A lot of the problem, I think, Clayton, has been, well, with the
trade publishers, a lot of the problem has been a failure of imagination where promotion was concerned for specific kinds of
books, as you well know. I think it was you, Kathleen, who indicated earlier that there might be a reluctance on the part of the
small-press people to share their lists. I have not found that to be
the case at all. I have found most of the small-press people to be
not only willing to share lists but also eager to do it and also eager to get into regional distribution, that kind of thing, on a cooperative basis. I don't think that the same kind of mentality that
operates against sharing in a number of other kinds of organizations that have something to do with literature—fund-raising organizations, for example—operates in this field at all. In the first
place, I think that poets by and large in this country are extraordinarily generous, sharing people, where information is concerned particularly. Fiction writers may be less so, because they
don't do readings and there is not a circuit in that sort of thing,
whereas poets have built up an enormous network of information

and circuits all around the country in various regions. But I think that the sharing of lists might be a good step in the right direction, if we can figure out a way to get them out and use them properly so it will do some good. Peter.

Peter Davison:

We have used Galen's poetry list. We've mailed out a postcard, signed by me, to everyone on the list that such-and-such a book is coming out. And I'm sorry to say I didn't notice an enormous increase in sales as a result, but this doesn't mean that the experiment was unsuccessful.

Williams:

About forty groups used our list last year, and we're now charging a little bit for it, trying to bring in some income, and we've gotten about eight requests so far, mostly from the big publishers.

Randolph:

Judy.

Judith Sherwin:

I've compiled a list of the Poetry Society of America, of seven hundred people who do occasionally buy poetry books. But I'd like to try to put some of the discussion together, for a moment, if I may, because it sounds as if you've all been attacking a possible project from different angles that are converging. Betty Kray has spoken about the lack of reliance that librarians place upon the poetry reviewing available. Kathleen Fraser and Galen Williams have talked about entire lists and amalgamating lists and marketing something through them. Yesterday James Laughlin talked about the long time it takes to keep a poetry book alive before it starts making the money. It sounds as if possibly one thing we want is for a sort of combination catalog and brief reviewing for all poetry books going out to all the people on all the lists, and offering a substantial discount for purchase of the books in the first three months or six months, or whatever it takes for them to exist long enough to get media attention on a wider scale.

Randolph:

Very good, Judith. I think that's basically what Kathleen was aiming at, probably, with the compilation of the list. That's what Betty was talking about when she was talking about the libraries, and that's exactly what Galen's been talking about now for the last four years, I guess, aiming in that direction.

Fraser:

My point was more than a list. It had to do with paranoia between small presses and big publishers, and I know that poets are very generous and that small-press people do a lot of sharing and supporting each other. But I bet if Doubleday asked Jack Shoemaker to share his list with them or vice-versa . . . I don't know, I'm just taking two arbitrary names.

Randolph:

Sure he would.

Fraser:

Okay, then it isn't obvious to me; I have never spoken to Jack about it. I'm basing my feeling on hanging around small-press people in northern California who have that East Coast-West Coast—you know, it's that strange kind of division.

Randolph:

It's just as bad on the East Coast.

Fraser:

Yeah. Well, I'm delighted if you think that it's that simple.

Randolph:

No, I think it could be done. No, I don't think there would be that much of a problem. I think that there might be a problem if you were talking about selling the list to any junk-mail dealer in the country. I think every small press would say no. But if you were saying that you wanted only to deal specifically with quality poetry and fiction that was going to be published by a reputable house, I have a feeling that they would not object. I have an idea that they would cooperate and they would be happy to, I suspect. I think most small-press people really have the feeling that we're all in this together. And if they don't, then they'd better start developing it, because we are, I'm afraid. And if one good small press kicks off someplace in the country, I think it really is the old John Donne thing all over again. I really do think it has an impact, an effect on other presses in other parts of the country—the same way with a good magazine. Betty, did you want to say something about that library thing? Did I misinterpret you?

Kray:

I just think that, to go back to reviewing, we have to go to a foundation to ask for money so that we can pay people. That's of great concern. But I think it has to start as somewhat selective. I just don't think you can review every book of poetry that's published. It is Grace's problem, as you all know, how to select, who selects, and all of that sort of thing. I just can't review books wholesale. It costs too much.

Randolph:

It probably—if you try to do everything, I think you would have a hard time doing it right away, anyway, Judy, but I suspect that the more people we can do, the more books we can review, the better off we're going to be. Yes, I agree with that, but initially you might have to limit it somewhat. Yes, Dan. Dan Hoffman.

Daniel Hoffman:

I'd like to add a comment to Betty Kray's account of her advising the librarians of Westerly, Rhode Island. I think anybody in this hall should constitute himself or herself a one-person advisory committee for the branch library or the hometown library nearest home. Librarians are really at sea in areas of literature with which they're not really familiar, and it's been my experience that they welcome informed comment from the readers in their libraries. And, furthermore, particularly public librarians and school librarians tend to order those books which they will then be able to show the boards of their libraries are actually circulating. And for this reason they waste public funds on cheap novels that are immediately made into movies and are really ninety-five-cent paperback material, and they get out and buy the $9.95 hardback edition. But in the meantime, what's happening to poetry books? If you read a book of poems that you really like, don't just be content to applaud it yourself, go and tell your librarian, "This is a book that belongs in the library." That's one of the things we can do. And I'd like you to know that the Academy of American Poets does publish a semiannual list of all the books by poets and the books about poetry, and these are valuable for later recommendations. If I may, I'd like to ask Ms. Ringer if she can tell us what the status of the copyright bill is at the moment, and how can we get hold of a copy of the bill, and to whom should we write if we wish to support parts of the bill?

Ringer:

I thank you for that question. The Senate full Judiciary Committee—all the stars, Senator Kennedy and so forth—acted on the
bill two weeks ago today and reported it favorably to the full Senate with a kind of a controversial amendment, which is a compulsory license that would involve poets and novelists. It is a compulsory—I really didn't intend to go into this, but I think I will sound
a word of warning. The so-called Mathias Amendment, which was
accepted, would allow public broadcasting—the other side of your
negotiations in the KTTV case—to use nondramatic literary and
musical works and pictorial, graphic, and sculptural works without
permission, upon payment into some kind of fund that would be
run out of the government, I presume out of my office, although
they're now talking about restructuring the procedure. This is
probably acceptable in the music field. There's an awful lot of
compulsory licensing and consent decrees and this and that in the
ASCAP-BMI situation. But it is the first time that an author
would literally lose control over a major primary use of his work,
and I don't think this has been sufficiently publicized. The bill is
still in the House. I'm the last witness in a series of long hearings
that have been going on all summer. I was the witness two weeks
ago Thursday on some of the problems we've been talking about
today, including library photocopying and educational uses, and
that was the fourteenth day of hearings. And apparently I'm going
to be testifying the day after tomorrow and again the following
Thursday, winding the hearings up, and then they will go on to a
markup. And I would say that the prognostications for enactment
by the middle of the summer are quite realistic. Is that enough
for now?

Hoffman:

How do we get hold of a copy of the bill?

Ringer:

Oh, I'm sorry. You can write to the Document Room in Congress, but by the time you get home and think about this, we
should have copies of the reported bill, which will include both
the bill itself and the explanation in the Senate, and I think this is
more valuable to you. You can look at it all in one document and
see the explanation of some of the sections, and you can write to
the Copyright Office for that.

Randolph:

Before I go on with the questions, I forgot to do something. I should insert in the record at this moment that the first question in this series was asked by Clayton Eshleman, the second was asked by Peter Davison, the third was asked by Judy Sherwin, and that was Daniel Hoffman. I'm supposed to ask you to give me your name when you ask a question. That's David Godine. What do you want, Dave?

Godine:

I strongly believe, everything tells me, that the real crisis in this country is not the trade publishers or that we don't have a great diversity of small presses. The real crisis in this country is much more, as we see it, a difficult cultural problem. It is essentially that people aren't reading, are not buying books. Now, that is the real problem, and when you approach that as a problem, I think you have the beginnings of a solution. Think of the statistic per person. Somebody's happy to have sold fifteen hundred copies of a poetry book: fifteen hundred copies out of 200 million people. And ten thousand copies of a poetry book, which would barely fill the east stands at Yankee Stadium, is a runaway best-seller. And I don't think it has to do with the very real problems of distribution. It has to do with the fact that publishing in this country is a small, small industry. We don't see it that way. We're all in it. We don't do it for our livelihood. It's tiny.

And the second point I want to make is that you have three ways to solve the problem. You can subsidize the producer of the books, which means that you can give money to the publishers and you can say, "Publish more books." You can subsidize the consumers of the books, which means you can go to a library and say, "Here's a hundred dollars, buy some poetry books." That, as has been proven again and again by what everyone has said here, is where the danger is. It is called "negative loss gain." The more poetry that is published in this country, the more money is lost publishing poetry. Right? No one on any of these panels has gotten up and said to our faces, "I'm making money publishing poetry or fiction or short stories." The more money that's going into it, the more money somebody is going to lose. And the third alternative is to influence the audience and to influence the marketplace. You use the tools at your disposal. In our case, unfortunately, those tools are TV, radio, media. We get the message to people that books are good things to own, good things to buy. Now, the people who do that for meat and potatoes, the people who do that for flowers, the people who do that for prunes, I think somebody can do that for books. And that's what's got to be done. The marketplace has to be influenced: not giving more money to somebody who needs to have his own so that he can publish another ten poems, not establishing a poetry collective that gets out fifty more poems, not even sharing lists, but influencing the marketplace. And my third suggestion is that if the way this conference was organized, the publicity it received, the promotion it received, the number of people you see sitting here in the seats, the number of people you see around you are any indication of the state of health of the publishing of fiction and poetry in this country, then we are in very, very sad shape, indeed.

Randolph:

Would you identify yourself, please?

Susan Wagner:

I'm with the Washington office of *Publishers Weekly,* and I've been covering the progress of copyright legislation through Congress for several years. And now we've moved into the brilliance of the furnace in this business, and I'll be writing about it almost all week. This week's issue has a story about the Mathias Amendment, and we'll follow up with reports on Barbara Ringer's very excellent testimony before the subcommittee. And so I think if you want to follow, blow by blow, the Authors' League proposals to Congress and so on, all the controversial aspects, I think you could get quite a bit of information out of *PW.*

Randolph:

The *Publishers Weekly* coverage on copyright in general, not only these hearings but over the past few years on the whole long, sad struggle involved—has been really incredibly good. Yes, Donald, I wish you would. Donald wants to speak to your point, David.

Barthelme:

I would like to disagree with David to this extent. I believe Americans love to read and read enormously. What you have is a situation in which two kinds of books are at war with each other. The greed of the commercial publishers is unimaginable. They are literally forcing the good books out of the bookstores. I have a friend who has just published an extra-special historical work, and he was horrified to learn that it was in Scribner's window on Fifth Avenue. And I thought he would be happy to learn this. He says, "No. The publication date is not until November 10, and if it's in Scribner's window now, the damn books will all be gone by the time the reviews come in." Gresham's law is frequently cited; it works beautifully. It's one of the best laws we have in terms of its effectiveness. The commercial publishers are so clogging the market that there is not room for the good stuff to live. For example, I might be vastly interested in the question of how to grow green plants. I might be, similarly, very interested in the question of how to make love well. These questions may have haunted me all my life, but in any given year, I'll be content with four books on each subject. We get sixty on each subject.

Randolph:

Especially on how to make love, not only well, but often. I think, David, I'd like to make just one brief comment about your use of the one million, whatever it was, dollar budget for ads on television. It won't go very far.

Godine:

We can't do it alone. We need the aid of TV to do that.

Randolph:

That's right. If you had a $25,000,000 budget, you might be able to have some impact on the marketplace, but only then. There was a question. Yes.

Eli Spark:

I live in Washington. David did not tag on at the end of his list the enormous void in our so-called educational system, which does not create a literate public with any cultural, literary, or a great many other interests. In this connection, it seems to me that some of the references to figures and situations in Sweden or Germany are quite irrelevant to our own concerns, because we are dealing with nations in which there is a higher literacy and a higher cultural interest and concern than there is in our own country. I'd like to ask Ms. Ringer a question. I'm sure in the society in which we have been told that the person yet unborn deserves sustenance and care and so forth, we all agree that poets and writers are creative people who are going to contribute something to our society and have as much right as anyone else to subsist. It's some comfort, perhaps, to have their time free so they can work and so forth. No doubt about that, to the extent one can do it within our system. I'd ask Ms. Ringer this: What is the difference, in connection with copyright and the technological changes here, from what exists, let's say, in the patent field, in which if Uncle Sam pays for a lot of research to produce something—discoveries and inven-

tions that have come out of it are in the public domain because the
taxpayers paid for it, to have something patentable, a person not
only must have been a serious scholar in a laboratory or been
writing long hours in his garret, but he must even, according to
our Supreme Court's famous decision, have invoked a spark of
creative genius. Now, what is the difference between the rewards
and relationships in that situation and that of the writer? Who'll
get the work, for example, provided for by this great overriding
system of our government, to which taxpayers are being pilfered
from and redistributed? Why should this not all be the public's
heritage at once? Bear in mind that the painter, for example, is
now busy writing contracts so that future increases in the value of
his product will be shared with him, I don't know how many years
hence. Michelangelo's heirs, I suppose, are entitled to some compensation for creation of high-quality color reproduction in art
books. I suggest that they'd probably feel much more honored in
the inheritance of Michelangelo. I suggest that society as a whole
is much more greatly enriched by that kind of thing than it is by
an elaborate government formula for taking care of reproductions
and divvying up pots and so forth.

Ringer:

I understand the point you're making. Let me observe that
there are patents and copyrights. As forms of intellectual property
they're recognized all over the world and are joined together in
holy wedlock in our Constitution. They're actually recognized.
Congress is charged with the responsibility of securing to authors
and inventors the exclusive rights in their respective writings and
discoveries. I've always felt that this was an interesting part of our
Bicentennial situation, but the patent law is a fairly effective law,
once you've got a patent. It's got an awful lot of things wrong
with it, and it doesn't do much to protect individual inventors. I
think it could do a great deal more, but it's not my field. My field
is copyright, and it does seem to me outrageous that anyone
should suggest that an author who is seeking a profession, probably the noblest there is, should be asked to donate the product of
his work, which is probably the hardest work there is, to the
"public," which is a bunch of ravening knock-off artists, when you
get right down to it.

Randolph:

I want to interrupt this. Hold on a second, please. Betty Kray
and Grace Schulman have to catch a plane, and we'll have to excuse them. Then we'll take another question.

Now, is there another question? Someone had his hand up a moment ago. Judith?

Sherwin:

I'd like to reply to David Godine, because I support him, except I think we should be using all the media we can lay our hands on. I think it would pay us to build up a larger readership, but I still think that that is not immediately in our power. What we can do is make a greater and more elaborately planned effort to meet the audiences that we personally know. Every poet here knows what our audiences are. Every fiction writer knows what the potential audience is, and if that audience is buying *Jaws*, the problem is not with their ability to read, it's what is put in front of them and what the price structure is. If the problem is keeping a book alive long enough for a demand to be developed for it, then what we want to do is offer a lower price for it in the first few months of its life and a higher price for people who wait around until the reviews hit the stands. If the publishing price structure is geared to that system, I think we may make a little headway. Now, I know Carol Bergé has done that with her magazine, which costs five dollars the first year an issue comes out, ten dollars the next year. And I think that works.

Randolph:

Thank you, Judy. All right, I want to thank all of you. I especially want to thank Stanley Kunitz and John Broderick and Nancy Galbraith for putting this conference together, all the members of the panels, all of the panels. I think perhaps David Godine is probably right, that we may have learned not enough out of this conference. I suspect we never will. I think we have found out a couple of things. Perhaps some of us attending this conference have found out a couple of things that we did not know before. I hope we have. I would hope, too, that those of you who have a continuing interest in literature and in the future of writers and in support for writers would try to come up with new ideas and new ways of doing better things, doing them more broadly and building audiences in literature throughout the entire country. I think unless all of us put our minds together and try a lot of things, some of which are going to be very high risk and very foolish, we're not going to be able to do very much about literature in America during the next five or ten years. But I do believe that, as Stanley said, there is a crisis, yes. I don't believe that we can make much headway just by saying that we're going to change either the marketplace or the education system, because we are very, very few, as David said, and they are very, very many, all of them. Try looking at the Office of Education Staff Directory, sometime, if you don't want to believe that. I think all of those things are right, but we have to do what we can do, as quickly as we can, and keep on doing it every year, no matter how it changes, no matter how frustrated we may get. That's what we've been trying to do these past two days, come up with a few suggestions, a few ideas, and I thank all of you for being very patient this afternoon and for being here in the first place. Thank you.

Don't forget, Donald Barthelme is reading tonight, here in the auditorium at eight o'clock. Is that right, Don? We had the question about fiction readers. Okay, now's your chance. You've got one of the best ones in the world tonight.

Other Publications on Literature Issued by the Library of Congress

Unless otherwise noted, these publications, based on lectures presented at the Library of Congress, may be purchased from the Superintendent of Documents, Government Printing Office, Washington, D.C. 20402. When ordering, please provide the title, date, and identifying number and enclose payment. Prices are subject to change.

American Poetry at Mid-Century. 1958. 49 p.*
New Poets and Old Muses, by John Crowe Ransom. The Present State of Poetry, by Delmore Schwartz. The Two Knowledges, by John Hall Wheelock.

Anni Mirabiles, 1921-1925: Reason in the Madness of Letters, by Richard P. Blackmur. 1956. 55 p.*
The Great Grasp of Unreason. The Techniques of Trouble. Irregular Metaphysics. Contemplation.

Anniversary Lectures, 1959. 1959. 56 p.*
Robert Burns, by Robert S. Hillyer. The House of Poe, by Richard Wilbur. Alfred Edward Housman, by Cleanth Brooks.

The Art of History: Two Lectures. 1967. 38 p. LC 29.9: N 41. 60 cents.
The Old History and the New, by Allan Nevins. Biography, History, and the Writing of Books, by Catherine Drinker Bowen.

Carl Sandburg, by Mark Van Doren. With a bibliography of Sandburg materials in the collections of the Library of Congress. 1969. 83 p. LC 29.9: V 28. $1.

Chaos and Control in Poetry: A Lecture, by Stephen Spender. 1966. 14 p. LC 29.9: SP 3/2. 55 cents.

---

* Out of print in this format, but reprinted in the collection *Literary Lectures Presented at the Library of Congress.*

159

Dante Alighieri. Three Lectures. 1965. 53 p. Out of print.
The Interest in Dante Shown by Nineteenth-Century American Men of Letters, by J. Chesley Mathews. On Reading Dante in 1965: The *Divine Comedy* as a "Bridge Across Time," by Francis Fergusson. The Relevance of the *Inferno*, by John Ciardi.

Edwin Arlington Robinson; a Reappraisal, by Louis Untermeyer. With a bibliography. 1963. 39 p.*

French and German Letters Today. 1960. 53 p.*
Lines of Force in French Poetry, by Pierre Emmanuel. Latest Trends in French Prose, by Alain Bosquet. Crossing the Zero Point: German Literature since World War II, by Hans Egon Holthusen. The Modern German Mind: The Legacy of Nietzsche, by Erich Heller.

From Feathers to Iron, by Stanley Kunitz. 1976. 16 p. LC 1.14: K 96. 35 cents.

From Poe to Valéry, by T. S. Eliot. 1949. 16 p.*

George Bernard Shaw, Man of the Century, by Archibald Henderson. 1957. 15 p.*

Germany and the Germans, by Thomas Mann. 1946. 20 p.*

Goethe and Democracy, by Thomas Mann. 1950. 28 p.*

Illusion and Reality, by Virginia Hamilton. 1976. 18 p. 50 cents.

The Imagination in the Modern World. Three Lectures, by Stephen Spender. 1962. 40 p.*
The Imagination as Verb. The Organic, the Orchidaceous, the Intellectualized. Imagination Means Individuation.

The Instant of Knowing, by Josephine Jacobsen. 1974. 14 p. LC 1.14: J 15. 35 cents.

Literary Lectures Presented at the Library of Congress. 1973. 602 p. LC 1.14: L 71. $8.50.
Reprints of 37 lectures on literature.

Louise Bogan: A Woman's Words, by William Jay Smith. With a bibliography. 1971. 81 p. LC 1.14: Sm 6. 95 cents.

Metaphor as Pure Adventure, by James Dickey. 1968. 20 p. LC 1.14: D 55/2. 40 cents.

---

*Out of print in this format, but reprinted in the collection *Literary Lectures Presented at the Library of Congress*.

National Poetry Festival, Held in the Library of Congress, October 22-24, 1962: Proceedings. 1964. 367 p. Out of print.

Nietzsche's Philosophy in the Light of Contemporary Events, by Thomas Mann. 1947. 37 p.*

Of Human Bondage, with a Digression on the Art of Fiction, by W. Somerset Maugham. 1946. 16 p. Out of print.

Perspectives: Recent Literature of Russia, China, Italy, and Spain. 1961. 57 p.*
    Russian Soviet Literature Today, by Marc Slonim. Chinese Letters since the Literary Revolution (1917), by Lin Yutang. The Progress of Realism in the Italian Novel, by Giose Rimanelli. The Contemporary Literature of Spain, by Arturo Torres-Rioseco.

Portrait of a Poet; Hans Christian Andersen and His Fairytales, by Erik Haugaard. 1973. 17 p. LC 29.9: H 29. 40 cents.

Questions to an Artist Who Is Also an Author: A Conversation between Maurice Sendak and Virginia Haviland. 1972. 18 p. LC 1.17/A:AR 78. 55 cents.
    Reprinted from the October 1971 *Quarterly Journal of the Library of Congress,* v. 28, no. 4.

Randall Jarrell, by Karl Shapiro. With a bibliography of Jarrell materials in the collections of the Library of Congress. 1967. 47 p. LC 29.9: Sh 2. 70 cents.

Recent American Fiction, by Saul Bellow. 1963. 12 p.*

Robert Frost: A Backward Look, by Louis Untermeyer. With a selective bibliography. 1964. 40 p. Out of print.

Robert Frost: Lectures on the Centennial of His Birth. 1975. 74 p. LC 1.4: T 18. $1.55.
    "In- and Outdoor Schooling"; Robert Frost and the Classics, by Helen Bacon. "Toward the Source"; the Self-Realization of Robert Frost, 1911-1912, by Peter Davison. Robert Frost's "Enigmatical Reserve"; the Poet as Teacher and Preacher, by Robert Pack. "Inner Weather"; Robert Frost as a Metaphysical Poet, by Allen Tate.

Saint-John Perse: Praise and Presence, by Pierre Emmanuel. With a bibliography. 1971. 82 p. LC 29.9: P 43. 90 cents.

Spinning the Crystal Ball; Some Guesses at the Future of American Poetry, by James Dickey. 1967. 22 p. LC 1.14: D 55. 40 cents.

---

* Out of print in this format, but reprinted in the collection *Literary Lectures Presented at the Library of Congress.*

Teaching Creative Writing. 1974. 135 p. LC 1.2: C 86. $1.40.

The Theme of the Joseph Novels, by Thomas Manr. 1943. 23 p.*

Three Views of the Novel. 1957. 41 p.*
   The Biographical Novel, by Irving Stone. Remarks on the Novel, by John O'-Hara. The Historical Novel, by MacKinlay Kantor.

The Translation of Poetry. Address by Allen Tate and panel discussion presented at the International Poetry Festival held at the Library of Congress, April 13-15, 1970. 1972. 40 p. LC 29.9: T 18. 60 cents.

Two Lectures. 1973. 31 p. LC 1.14: ST 1. 55 cents.
   Leftovers: a CARE Package, by William Stafford. From Anne to Marianne: Some Women in American Poetry, by Josephine Jacobsen.

Walt Whitman: Man, Poet, Philosopher. 1955, reissued 1969. 53 p. LC 29.2: W 59/2. 65 cents.
   The Man, by Gay Wilson Allen. The Poet, by Mark Van Doren. The Philosopher, by David Daiches.

The War and the Future, by Thomas Mann. 1944. 23 p.*

Ways of Misunderstanding Poetry, by Reed Whittemore. 1965. 13 p.*

Willa Cather: The Paradox of Success, by Leon Edel. 1960. 17 p.*

The Writer's Experience. 1964. 32 p.*
   Hidden Name and Complex Fate: A Writer's Experience in the United States, by Ralph Ellison. American Poet? by Karl Shapiro.

U.S. GOVERNMENT PRINTING OFFICE: 1977 O—227-180